Daddy's Big Girl

T.R. Baker

Copyright © 2013 by T.R. Baker
2nd Edition © 2016 T.R. Baker

Library of Congress Control Number: 2016915618

ISBN-10: 0-9857647-2-4
ISBN-13:978-0-9857647-2-2

1. African-American women – Fiction. 2. Family life – Fiction.

Dedicated with Love
Emma L. Baker & Willie Baker Jr.

(Mama & Daddy)

Daddy's Big Girl

Even now, in a room full of people
she feels like a child
A shy demure little daddy's girl
Will she ever grow up
Does she want to grow up

Staring at a chandelier she sees
sparkling diamonds that belong only to her,
given to her by her daddy

He was the first
…to tell her she was beautiful
…to tell her she was intelligent
…to clap when she gave private concerts, out of tune

Her daddy,
flawless in every way
Protector, vindicator, and provider
Jack of many trades, mastering them all
in the eyes of a daddy's girl

Lack luster in her love for any man
'cause no man is like her daddy
…who could plant a flower garden
and make a game of it
…who could wake her up at six in the morning
to enjoy the morning dew
…who could play circus with her
and fly her on his feet,
that miraculously became a flying trapeze
Who could ever be like her Don Juan, her guardian, her
Superman
…her hero

Standards of a man, a husband, a father, a friend
too high for mere mortal men to ever meet
Lessons of love and family strong and binding
Seeking to be treated like the princess that she is
Wanting to always hear

…that she's beautiful
…that she's intelligent
…that she's a daddy's girl

Daddy's Big Girl

Also by T.R. Baker
Every Time I Close My Eyes

ACKNOWLEDGMENTS

Thank you to Pamela Williams for making me feel like a New York Times Best Sellers' List author; Willa Dickerson for falling in love with Hayes; Leatha Griffin Gallon for allowing me to read to you; Alex Malone, Chaz Cross, Cassandra Myers for (sort of) reading the rough draft; Gwyn Brown for my desperate photo shoot; Gudrun Hughes for all of the great notes and for reminding me to pay attention to the details; and Keith Saunders of Marion Designs for the cover (which almost gave me a nervous breakdown, that I don't think he knew about).

To those who encouraged me, a long time ago (2003), after my first book: Circle of Friends, who invited me to my very first literary event; Raw Sistahs, for telling me to work on "dialogue," Page Turners Book Club, A Book and a Biscuit, and Onyx, for inviting me to your meetings as a guest author.

For continued moral and technical support from Black Writers with Purpose and the Atlanta Writers' Club, thank you.

A special thank you to: "Not Until My Wedding Night," Essence Magazine, Lakita Garth; "Loving the Older Man," Essence Magazine, Nadira A. Hira; NPR/How to Become a Marriage Educator/Adult Children of Divorce; "Beat the Odds: Make Your Marriage Work Despite Your Parents' Divorce," Beverly & Tom Rodgers; and Michael Vincent Miller, PhD., "Intimate Terrorism," The Oprah Magazine.

And THANK YOU to: Mint Condition, Kindred the Family Soul, and Raphael Saadiq for the background music that kept me in the moment, and everyone else that encourages me to continue writing.

Chapter 1

The day started off like any other typical day. As I drove, I found myself releasing the day's woes by trying to figure out what was so important that I had to stop by my parents' house before going home after work. *Mom and Dad are finally going to sell the house.* That had to be it. As I exited the car, nothing seemed any different. Once inside the house the atmosphere was welcoming, with that little hint of understated tension. It hadn't always been like that. I recalled a time when the Bassett home was always warm and inviting. If asked, I could probably tell you exactly when it changed. I entered the house oblivious to the possibility that this visit could be any different than any of my other visits home. Why would it be?

At 5'10", my long strides led me quickly through the foyer into the living room, where I found both of my parents. My mother sat comfortably on the couch; my father stood as I entered the room. He walked over to me and welcomed me with a tight hug and a kiss on the cheek. I walked over to my mom and placed a kiss on her cheek before taking a seat next to her.

I quickly examined their faces. "Why so serious? What's going on?"

My dad was the first to speak. "Your mom and I…we're getting a divorce."

Before I knew it, I had jumped to my feet. "What do you mean you're getting a divorce? Daddy, that's crazy!

1

I quickly turned to look at my mother. "What is he talking about?"

"Vada Jade, sit back down and let your father finish talking."

"VJ, baby, your mom and I haven't been happy for some time now, so I'm moving out. Actually, I moved out last week. I wanted to be the one to tell you, but your mom thought we should talk to you together. I know it's difficult for you to understand right now, but I assure you, I love both you and your mother. So, it's not about that. It's just that we, your mom and I, have grown in different directions over the years and it's best that we go on with our lives…separately."

Sobbing, I turned and looked at my mother. "What is he talking about? This is just crazy; it's the most ridiculous thing I've ever heard. Why in the world would y'all be getting divorced after 40 years? Dad, is there another woman involved?"

"Vada, I'm not here to discuss details with you. It doesn't matter."

Unable to contain myself, I screamed, "What do you mean it doesn't matter? It does matter. Everything matters right now..."

"Vada Jade, you need to not only lower your voice but change your tone, as well. You're still talking to your father." Mom could tolerate a lot from me, but not disrespect.

Mom and Dad sat quietly, gazing at me. They knew how I'd react and just as they had expected, their 33-year-old daughter, the attorney, ranted, raved, and pouted. Mother actually appeared totally detached from the scene I was making. After all, she had known for some time that her husband was going to leave; she just didn't know when. Years of dealing with emotional, sometimes overly emotional, patients prepared her for my emotional tirade, and then there was the common knowledge that I always reacted dramatically when it came to my daddy.

The look on my father's face said more than his words could ever say; he knew he was in the wrong. At 58 years old he had decided to start a new family and a new life. He knew I would never understand, and I'm sure he worried that I'd never forgive him. There was no doubt he was more concerned with what I might think than he was with what my mom thought. What he didn't know was how his decision to start anew would forever alter how I felt about him, and perhaps any other man that would now come into my life.

———

March 4, 2012

This is the first time that I've sat down to write since Friday. Where do I begin, at the beginning I suppose? Most significant event last week: My dad left us. He said he was moving out. Actually, he said he had already moved out. Words cannot begin to express what I feel right now…pain, dismay, disappointment, bewilderment. Did I already say disappointment? I've never experienced these feelings all at one time, I don't think. So, I don't know what to call it. At least, today isn't as intense as it was the other day and I'm not nauseous anymore. Daddy openly shared his insanity with the world (it's okay to be crazy – you just have to keep your madness to yourself sometimes). It feels like someone very close to me has died.

This whole situation has me absolutely sick. I'm an intelligent person. I know how this came about, but I still don't understand what's going on. I'm at a loss as to what to do or what to say to my mother. I suppose all of us played a role in this somehow. I'm just not sure what role I played. I think, not acknowledging the things I saw was not the right thing to do. I guess silence counts for something too. But what was I supposed to do?

I haven't talked with my mom since Friday. I don't know what to say to her. Even if we did talk, I don't think I could hold myself together long enough to say anything worthwhile. I wonder how she's doing…really? What's going to happen to her now; does she have to grow old alone? I'm not sure what I saw when I looked at her. She's hard to read because she's always so stoic. Now that I think about it, when I look back, I can remember a few times when her conversation and her actions were a bit erratic, but I attributed it to her personal eccentricities, not to my dad – not the dad of all dads and the husband of all husbands. I can't stop crying on the inside...

THANKFUL FOR: waking up in good health this morning.

―――――

I had originally planned to take the week off, but I knew I would do little more than play the conversation with my dad over and over in my head like a broken record. So, instead, I thought it better to just immerse myself in my work – the week would go by quicker that way. The part of me that always fought back told me to slough it off and stop acting like a baby. That same part also told me to take home as much work as possible, so that I'd have an excuse to avoid talking with my mother, as well as anyone else.

The intercom buzzed and startled me.

"Yes."

"VJ, it's Mr. Townes. Would you like for me to transfer him to you?"

"Yes, thank you, Carolyn."

As I waited for the call to come through, I quickly flipped through a brief that was on my desk.

"Hi, William."

"Hey, baby, what're you doing for lunch?"

"William, I have so much work, I don't know if I have time for lunch today."

"I'll be there at 11:30. Meet me out front."

"William, really I can't..."

"See you at 11:30, sweetness."

I hated when he did that, ignored what I was saying. As much as I hated it, he did it so often I'd almost come to expect it. The more I thought about it, though, the better lunch sounded. Maybe an hour or two away from the office would do me some good. I also convinced myself that lunch would be the best venue to talk with

William about why I hadn't felt like seeing him for the last few days.

I glanced up at my door just as Hayes Vishmell passed by. Without a shadow of a doubt, he's the most handsome partner with the firm – he's the handsome, dark chocolate, distinguished looking partner with the firm, to be exact. The phrase "rugged and strong" always comes to mind when I see him – every time I see him. His bowlegs and his slow stride made me and Dee dub him "the chocolate cowboy." Seeing him usually drew out a school girl's giddiness from me, but today seeing him wasn't even enough to take me out of my misery. He looked right into my eyes and, for a change, there was no comforting sensation. I felt as though I was standing naked and exposed. I quickly averted my gaze and looked down at my desk. I wondered if he was aware he had the power today.

———

As soon as I closed the car door William began to do what he does.

"Ms. Bassett, you look delicious, as usual."

"Thanks, William. To what do I owe this pleasure?"

"What do you mean? I missed you."

"What do you mean you missed me? It's not like we have lunch together every day. Where're we going anyway?"

"What are you in the mood for, sweetness?"

I didn't feel much like eating, so I didn't care what we ate. "How 'bout Italian?"

"I don't know, V."

"Well, what do you want?"

"I think I'm feeling like Jamaican."

"If my honey wants Jamaican, then Jamaican it is," I chimed in.

As William drove he held my hand and talked. About what, I had no idea. I could hear him speaking, but my mind was far away. We arrived at Jamaica Breeze in just a few minutes. William pulled up to the curb and asked me if I'd get us a table. While he parked the car I thought about my mom: *Maybe I should call her tonight. I don't want to talk about the divorce, though. I just need to see how she's doing.* As I waited for the hostess to call us for our table, William walked up behind me and grabbed my hand.

His eyes searched my face. "What are you thinking about?"

"Huh? I'm sorry. What did you say?"

William shook his head. "Don't worry about it. It looks like our table is ready."

Once we were seated, our server took our drink orders very quickly.

Leaning across the table, William whispered, "So, what have you been doing all week that you couldn't call a brother back? You're not seeing someone else, are you?"

I was baffled that he would even jokingly ask me something like that. "There have been plenty of times when you've been unavailable to talk with me. As a matter of fact, there have been times when you haven't

7

seen me for days at a time, and I've never asked you anything like that. I would think you'd know better."

"Girl, you know I'm not serious. But for real, what's been going on with you?" His question was clearly a feeble attempt to mask what he was really thinking.

A restaurant was not the place for emotional conversation, so I strongly considered whether or not I should mention my parents' situation. William and I hadn't even eaten yet. I quickly came to the conclusion that now was as good a time as any.

"My parents are getting a divorce."

"If you don't want to tell me what you've been doing you don't have to, but don't make up stuff, V."

Tears began to puddle in my eyes. "Really, they are. Last Friday I went home to see them and they sat me down and told me they were getting a divorce. My dad has already moved out."

"That's deep. Maybe it's for the best."

These would be the only words of encouragement that William could come up with. I didn't understand why he would say that. Particularly, since he, better than anyone, with the exception of Dee, knew what kind of relationship I had with my parents. Maybe his view of marriage was slightly skewed because his father cheated on his mother for years.

"You honestly think, after being married for forty years, this might be for the best?"

As I looked at him I realized William didn't have a clue.

Before he could respond, I continued, "Maybe you're right, William. Maybe you're right…"

Chapter 2

Back at work I sat behind the stacks of paper and files on my desk. *Maybe William didn't understand what I was saying. He couldn't have. He doesn't understand the impact all of this has on me – on my little psyche. My mother and father are my foundation; they're supposed to be together forever, however long that might be. What are my children going to do now? What was my father thinking? How could he do this?* Just as I made up my mind to work from home for the remainder of the day, my phone rang.

"Yes…"

"Hey girl, what'cha wanna do tonight?" It was Delaney "Dee" Brown-Lofton, my best friend, who just happened to also work at the law firm.

"Why, Dee, what do you want to do?"

"Let's go to happy hour somewhere, have a couple of drinks, and eat some free food."

I sighed heavily before responding. "I really don't feel like it tonight."

"Why, William coming over? You'll be home long before he gets there."

"Excuse me. Do I sense some sarcasm in your voice?"

"Yep, you certainly do!"

"I don't know why you don't like him. He likes you…"

Before I could finish, Dee abruptly interrupted. "Uh,

huh, I'm sure he does."

It was no secret that there was bad blood between Dee and William. She hasn't cared for him since the night we all first met at a mutual friend's party. Her exact words to me were, "That brother is high maintenance. He's 'too' pretty." What bothered her the most that night was that he had come to the party with a date but left with my phone number. That fact didn't escape me either, nor did it bother me. He explained that the young lady was just a date for the party. At the time, I had no reason to question that. As far as I was concerned, I wanted him to have my telephone number.

Dee, on the other hand, spent the balance of the evening and the entire ride home trying to convince me that he was not worth my time or energy.

"Do you want to go to happy hour or what, VJ?"

"I was just getting ready to leave. I think I'm going to finish working from home. Why don't you come over after work? We can order in and, if you must drink, you know my bar is fully stocked; how about that?"

"Okay, but it won't be the same. Nobody will be able to see how cute I am if we drink at your house."

"Girl, you're crazy. See you at the house." I shook my head as I hung up the phone.

The conversation did at least manage to cheer me up. It momentarily took my mind off of my parents…and lunch with William.

———

I began to look for my garage door opener as I turned

into my driveway. I wondered out loud why I just didn't put the stupid thing on my visor after I used it and why I had to have this conversation with myself every day. I eventually found the thing on the floor, underneath my seat. Once I was in the garage, I lowered the door and sat there for a minute gathering my things to take in the house with me. Out of nowhere, I began to bawl like a baby.

A wave of thoughts flooded my mind; the foremost of which was how selfish my father was. I eventually pulled myself together – fifteen minutes, or so, later. As I opened the door leading to the laundry room, I decided I'd have that drink that Dee had talked about earlier.

———

March 9, 2012

Why am I taking this so personally? I'm a grown woman. Maybe William is right. Maybe it is for the best…and I just can't see it right now. My mom didn't seem to be bothered by this as much as I am…and I just can't seem to pull myself together. It's consuming my every thought. I suppose I should really talk to somebody about this – William doesn't count. He's just no good with this kind of family stuff. He's a sweet guy – very attentive, affectionate, respectful, and loving, but I have to admit, we have somewhat different definitions of family and family values. In spite of that, one of these days I'm sure we'll get married. I wonder if "he'll" just up and leave me and our children when he turns 60? The bigger question is: Will I still be so unhappy with my father that I won't want him to walk me down the aisle? Or what about, will I allow him to bring the other woman to my wedding? Okay, I think I'm going over the deep end. William and I aren't even engaged and I'm tripping about a wedding. I think I should stop here and have that drink.

THANKFUL FOR: having a mom and a dad

———

By the time Dee arrived I had changed into a big T-shirt and a pair of sweat pants and was working on my second, strong pomegranate martini. Dee let herself in and hollered out as she made her grand entrance through the kitchen.

"I'm here."

She found me sitting on the couch in the family room, so she walked over and greeted me with a kiss on the cheek.

"What is that in your hand? I thought you were coming home to work. Who was it that said they didn't feel like drinking tonight?"

With a smirk on my face, I looked up at her. "No, what I said was, I didn't feel like going to happy hour. You interpreted that as I didn't want to drink. Just fix yourself something and be quiet, if you can."

We both laughed as she walked over to the bar.

Dee took a knowing look back at me before picking up a glass. "Okay, so what's up with you? I've been trying to give you a little space to work it out. When William is involved, I know you need 'as much air' as possible."

"Dee, in spite of what you might believe, William is not the center of my world. Everything is not about him, you know?" I slurred just a little as I spoke.

"Uh, huh…"

"What? It's not!"

Dee walked over to the loveseat across from me. Kicking off her black, patent leather, Prada pumps, she sipped her drink of choice, Jack Daniels on the rocks with a splash of coke, as she folded her legs underneath her and sat down.

"If it's not William, then what is it? Oh, and please stop slurring. It's rude."   Excitedly, Dee went on, "Please tell me you're tormented because you've found someone else and you don't know how to tell him? I'll talk with him if you want me to. I know how to let the brotha' down easy." Dee took a sip from her drink and then smacked her lips.

I took the cherry from my glass and popped it into my mouth before nonchalantly announcing, "Mr. and Mrs. Bassett are getting a divorce."

"Mr. and Mrs. Bassett who?" Dee stopped what she was doing and fixed her eyes on me.

"My mom and dad; who do you think?"

Dee sat up straight. Choking on her drink, she struggled to speak. "VJ, no, not Mama and Daddy Bassett. What happened?" She put her drink on the table and walked over to the couch and sat next to me. "Are you all right?"

I quickly jumped to my feet and walked toward the bar to avoid the forthcoming hug, which would do little more than push me over the edge, emotionally. Dee somehow always managed to be there for me – and this time, of course, would be no different. Anything good or bad, happy or sad and Dee was right there grinning, laughing, crying, talking trash, or sitting quietly. She was, by far, the best friend anyone could ask for. In spite of that, a hug was not what I wanted at that moment. I wasn't really sure what I wanted. So, I put on a brave face which, at that moment, was easy for me to do since I was working on my third really strong drink.

"It's okay, Dee. I've talked with them and this isn't a spontaneous decision that they've made. It's my understanding that it's something that's been coming for years now."

Dee knew me as well as she knew herself. I'm sure she believed she was familiar with every face that her friend could put on. As I stood at the bar making my next martini, she got up from the couch and began to walk toward me.

"VJ, if you don't want to, we don't have to talk about this right now." She softly touched my arm. "Sweetie, are you going to be all right though?"

I whipped around so quickly that it startled her. What seemed to alarm Dee even more was the fact that she wasn't able to read what was going to happen next.

As I sipped from my glass, I smacked my lips in approval. "Dee, I'm fine. These things happen."

———

When morning rolled around I didn't even remember falling asleep on the couch, nor did I remember Dee leaving. My first thought, though, was that I didn't feel like taking a shower, but I would at least brush my teeth. As I drug myself into the kitchen and looked around, I needed to eat something because I had a horrible hangover, but I didn't feel like going through the motions of cooking. As I walked through the kitchen to my bedroom, it occurred to me that the morning sun was extremely bright, so I took a quick glance at the clock on the counter. It was going on 1 o'clock in the afternoon. I was shocked because I'm always up before 7 o'clock in the morning.

The phone seemed to ring non-stop from 2:00 p.m. to 10:00 p.m. I didn't bother answering it, though. The last time I looked there were twelve messages. I wasn't in the mood to talk to anybody: not my mom, my dad, William, or Dee; and, anyway, lying in the fetal position on the couch under my favorite afghan was far too comfortable. It was like being in my mom and dad's bed. I smiled as I mused to myself. Even in my thirties, I could always count on going to my parents' home and lying across the foot of their bed, talking with them as they dozed off. It gave me a sense of comfort. The phone rang again, but the previous evening's libations were still demanding immobility. How many pomegranate martinis had I drunk anyway? I couldn't recall. I had lost count after four.

Okay, my dad is going on with his life. What exactly

does that mean for us, for me and my mom? Does that now mean I'm no longer a part of his life? Okay, okay…so, those Sundays when I went home and he wasn't there, he was with some other woman? My mind couldn't wrap around the last thought.

As I began to cry, yet again, I wanted to scream out irrationally, like a child. I knew that was ridiculous, but at 33 years old my broken heart couldn't take it any longer. So, I sought a safe space in my mind and finally fell asleep.

Chapter 3

Sunday morning seemed to come around too quickly. Even though I woke up with a new attitude, surprisingly, I still had a hangover. As I sat on the edge of the couch, I went over my agenda for the day: shower and wash my hair; put on clean clothes; start a load of laundry; put dirty glasses in the dishwasher; call my mother; call Dee; cook dinner; and, finally, call William to invite him over for dinner. As I made my way through the day, I was determined to stop feeling sorry for myself. I knew I was being ridiculous. It was my mother that was getting the divorce. *The coming week would be better than the previous week* – I was convinced of that. *After all, you can only take it one day at a time.* Next call to order was to get in contact with my mother.

"Good morning, Mom."

When she said hello, she sounded glad to hear my voice, but that didn't last long.

"Vada Jade, where have you been? Are you all right? I had made up my mind to come over there if I didn't hear from you today."

"Mom, I'm fine. You know how I am. I had to think some things through. I apologize for not calling sooner."

"I hope you weren't hold up in the house all weekend thinking about me and your daddy?"

"To be honest with you, I was and I did…all weekend. I am so disappointed in Daddy. You know, when I was in school I remember having friends whose parents weren't together. It always felt good to know that my parents were still married to each other. Goodness, when I talked with other kids whose dads had other families, I felt privileged to have a dad that didn't sleep around. Now my dad is one of those dads. He's just like anybody else now…common. Sorry, Mom, I told myself I wasn't going to go there today."

"Vada, sweetheart, I wish I knew what to say to make things better, but I don't. I guess that's because I'm going through this too. Like I told you last week, emotionally your dad left this house and our marriage years ago; his body finally decided to go with him. It took him that long to get up the nerve, I suppose. I knew it was happening and I wondered when it would actually take place, but, to be honest with you, I don't know that I really thought it was going to ever happen."

"You know what makes me maddest, Mom? He's going on with his life and starting over, like we've lost our usefulness. But more importantly, he's left you to grow old by yourself. I just don't understand that, after 40 years."

"Well, if you figure it out then you should write a book about it because it happens all of the time. You'd certainly become a very wealthy woman. This too shall pass, though. Look, you want to come over for dinner tonight?"

Suddenly I was feeling trapped. Already, I was beginning to feel the pressure of being the one that had to be there for my mother. As an only child, it wasn't like I wasn't the one with that responsibility anyway, but for some strange reason it now felt a little different.

"I had planned on inviting William over because I didn't spend any time with him last week. Can we do dinner some time during the week, maybe even tomorrow night?" I grimaced as I spoke.

I was sure Mom's intent was to get me out of the house, so that I wouldn't be alone. Having William over for dinner would suffice. It would keep me from sulking over the divorce.

"That's fine, sweetheart. Give me a call and let me know what we're going to do."

"Thanks, Mom."

"Tell William I said hello."

"I will."

"I'll talk with you later, VJ."

———

I didn't really want to get into a long drawn out conversation with Dee, but I felt I owed her, at least, a phone call to let her know that I was amongst the living. She had left seven messages. I was actually surprised that she hadn't come over, forced her way into my house, and insisted that I pull myself together. As I prepared to dial the phone it rang.

"Quincy, boy, if you don't stop making all of that noise... Hello?"

"Hey, Dee."

Dee's voice livened up as soon as she realized I was on the phone. "Hey, girl, are you okay? I was really starting to get worried about you. If I didn't hear from you today, the little boy and I were going to come over and check on you."

"I'm all right," I chuckled. "I apologize for worrying you."

Dee laughed. "Are you raggedy and stank? You were tore up Friday night. I have never, ever, seen you that drunk in my life."

I echoed her laughter. "Not any more. I couldn't take it. I had to finally get in the shower."

"VJ, Quincy and I would love to have you over for dinner tonight. You probably need to get out of the house, you know?"

"Sorry, but I…"

"I know. You're having dinner with William, right?"

"Yep, I still have to call him, but that's the plan." I knew that wouldn't sit well with her. It never does.

Dee whined on, "VJ, why can't you just have dinner with us tonight and do something with your little honey tomorrow night?"

"Why do we have to go through this every single time that I tell you I have plans with William?"

"Uh, perhaps because…I don't like him, I don't know. Why do you think?"

"All right, this is what I'll do. I will give William a call and if he's not available for dinner tonight then I'll come over and have dinner with Quincy. I don't know if I really want to be bothered with you."

"Whatever! We look forward to seeing you when you get here."

As soon as I ended the call the phone rang.

"Hello."

"Hey, sweetness, just calling to check on you; how are you?"

"William, your ears must be burning. Dee and I were just talking about you."

"I hope it was all good?"

"Look, what are you doing later on? I'd like to get with you for dinner." I purposely avoided answering his question.

"Ooh, I don't know, baby. You know the restaurant is busy on Sunday evenings. I don't think I can get away for dinner tonight. I could probably come by after I close up, though."

"William, I really want to spend some time with you tonight. I need you here to hold me…"

"Sweetness, I wish I could. You know I do."

"Okay, whatever, William."

"Don't be like that. Don't be mad, baby. I said I could come over after I close up."

"No, I think I'll just have dinner with Dee and Quincy. It'll probably be late when I get back home and tomorrow is a workday. Unlike you, my workday begins at 8:30 every morning, not at lunch time or whenever I decide to show up."

"I'll call you when I get off. If you're home I'll come over."

"William…"

———

"Auntie VJ, I'm glad you came over to see me."

"I'm glad too, Quincy."

"Mama said to be extra nice to you because you were sad. You still sad?"

How could I stay sad when I looked at Quincy's smile or recollected all of the funny stories that he told me during dinner? Nothing beats being entertained by a five year old.

"Okay, boy, let's get you in the bathtub, so you can get your bath and then go to bed," Dee ordered him.

"Please, can I stay up and talk with Auntie VJ?"

"Nope, you know I don't play that. Tomorrow is a school day and I don't want you crying because you're too sleepy to get up. Dad, can you come get this boy and put him in the tub and get him ready for bed?"

Dee's dad stays with her and he's the best live in grandfather and babysitter anybody could ask for. She wouldn't have it any other way. After her mother died, he raised her and her brother and sister by himself – he never remarried. He retired a few years ago and moved in with Dee after her divorce. They needed each other, so it worked out perfectly.

Dee and I sat and talked for another hour or so.

As Dee flipped through TV stations, she asked me a question that she had to know would only lead to an argument.

"So, what did Mr. Townes say when you told him about your parents' divorce? You did tell him, right?"

"Where did that come from?" My left eyebrow unconsciously rose.

"He's your man. So, it would only make sense that

you looked to him for a little support. Would that be an incorrect assumption on my behalf, Counselor?"

"It would be incorrect to assume anything, but, for your information, I did mention it to him…"

"…and?"

"If you just let me finish, I'll tell you. He thought it might be for the best."

Dee stopped fiddling with the remote control and looked at me. "What did he mean by that; the best for whom?" She sighed heavily. "That's just like him. He's so simple. I will never understand why you even fool with him." She shook her head and turned her attention back to the TV.

"The beauty of this is you don't have to understand it. It's just your job to love and support me as a friend. If I had it my way, my best friend and my man would get along, but since y'all don't and it doesn't seem like it's going to change any time soon, I guess I just have to deal with it." I wrinkled my nose at her.

"I guess so." The look of consternation on Dee's face spoke volumes.

"What's that look for?"

"Nothing, I was just agreeing with you."

I stood up and went for my purse and jacket. I thought it best that I leave before we became embroiled in our monthly 'Dee hates William Morris Townes' diatribe.

"Well, girl…I better go on home. You know as well as I do, tomorrow is a workday. Have to go and get ready to play the game, right?"

"I remember back when we could stay up all night, and then get up and go straight to class the next morning. What happened to us?"

I looked at her and smiled. "What happened to us? You got married, had a baby, and got old."

As she stood up, Dee hit me on the thigh with the remote control. "You say that like I'm getting old by my doggone self? I bet you I can still pull an all-nighter with the best of them."

"Yep, and an all-day 'broke down' would come right after that."

We both laughed as we walked to the door.

Chapter 4

"VJ, I know you're worried about me, but I'm fine, honey. Your dad and I had some really great years together. We learned a lot from each other. I'm not going to sit here and tell you that I completely understand what happened or that I approve of it, but in a self-healing way I do accept it because I want to move on. Am I sad? Of course I am. Am I angry? I just lost my husband of 40 years and a man that was originally my best friend. Of course I'm angry, but I'm tired too.

On some of those weekends when you came by I'm sure you noticed your dad wasn't here. You had to know he wasn't working all the time. It started with him, occasionally, not coming home at night. Then it escalated to him not coming home for a weekend or two a month, and then, finally, to him not coming home for an entire week at a time. I'm not going to go into all of the sordid details, but he and I talked and in the beginning it seemed like whatever it was it was going to run its course."

"But, Mom, why didn't you ever talk with me? I hate that you suffered through that by yourself."

"First of all, you're my child, not my friend. I stayed busy and I talked about it with my friends, some of whom had experienced the same thing in their marriages. Initially, I thought it was a phase that he was going through. That he would burn himself out and come back home. He wouldn't have been the same man I fell in love with all those years ago, but he would have been my husband again. I started realizing that whatever it was, or better yet, whoever she was, it was a little more than just a frivolous fling."

"Why didn't you just ask him about her?"

"Honey, let me tell you something about a cheating man, because that's what your daddy was, is, or whatever, but uhm, he's not going to tell you the truth. If he'll cheat, he's prepared to lie. If I had asked him about her he would have tried to convince me that I was the reason he was cheating. So, after approaching him a few times, I left it alone. I knew he was lying. I had to maintain my own emotional well-being and prepare myself for the worst. I still don't know if I did the right thing. I kept myself very busy, so I didn't have to constantly face the situation or him, for that matter. Eventually, enough was enough. I told him I was going to file for divorce because I wasn't going to live my life out like that."

I really wanted to ask my mother if she used a condom when she was with him, but I knew that was crossing a line I did not care to broach. It wasn't like I was talking with Dee. The idea of my dad having sex with another woman, and then coming home to my mother, disgusted me. As a matter of fact, the very idea of my parents having sex was like a nether world concept to me. I smiled to myself at my childishness.

Mom and I talked for another couple of hours. I listened more than anything else because I wanted to hear one word from her mouth that would make me understand the situation better. I never heard it, but I did find peace of mind. I came to recognize that my mother was okay. Her confidence and strength was the same familiar confidence and strength that most Black women exude, in spite of being betrayed. Historically, we have learned to endure almost anything. My mother had, seemingly, overcome the adversity of her situation. Now I would have to figure out how to draw from that same reservoir of hope.

The comfort I found from my mother's words helped me to understand that not only were things going to be okay in the near future, things were actually already okay. I just needed to find a way to accept the new reality of our family. For the next two hours our words filled the air around me like incense. The more we talked the easier I found it to acknowledge this foible in life and move on. I left my mother's house having a newfound respect for this woman I called Mother...Mom. I hope one day I can become half the woman she is, instead of the lost little girl I feel like now.

We laughed from our bellies when Mom managed to throw a few funny memories into the conversation. She reminded me of the shopping trips she and I would go on without my dad, which wasn't very often. When we got back home I would always rush into the house and Daddy would plant himself on the couch. I would then make the living room my own personal catwalk, as I modeled each new outfit for him. Sometimes he even took pictures while I stopped and posed for the camera.

That was one of my fondest memories; he was the first man to ever make me feel beautiful.

———

March 26, 2012

Yesterday Mom and I finally talked. Neither one of us mentioned the divorce during dinner. We actually talked about my job and about William (which was baffling because she didn't talk about him that often. I really don't think my mother likes him that much, but that's for another journal entry). After dinner we sat in the den and watched TV and talked some more.

We eventually started talking about my father. I kept telling her how worried I was, even though she seemed to have a handle on things. She eloquently quashed all of that. Here I was thinking she was devastated by him leaving and the more I talked with her the more I realized it was all "in my mind." She actually seemed to be doing better than me. I can't imagine the initial pain, though – 40 years is a long time. If I hadn't been so self-absorbed we could have talked sooner…

THANKFUL FOR: BLACK WOMEN

Chapter 5

A few weeks had past and I was still dragging myself into work every day, hoping each day would end almost as quickly as it began. I dreaded even more the idea of talking with clients, current or perspective. With each male client or attorney that I spoke with, I found myself wondering if he had ever cheated on his wife or girlfriend. Dee told me I was being silly and that I had no reason to question the fidelity of every single man in existence. I knew that, but I had neither found a way to nor had I allowed myself to move beyond being ridiculous. As difficult as it was for me to come to terms with, the definition of man, father, and husband did not begin or end with my dad. Both Dee and I laughed when she told me that. I couldn't believe what I was doing to myself. I hoped my emotional state wouldn't impact my relationship with William, but I found myself almost not caring. He wasn't being the most supportive boyfriend anyway.

Then there's that Hayes Foreman Vishmell. He's actually the best part of any given day at the office, and the only man I could actually tolerate thinking about. With his 52-year-old, 6'5", black self; the man was just plain, old fashion fine. His slightly bowed legs didn't take anything away from him either. I knew it was crude, but I had on occasion gotten up and gone to my door just to watch him walk down the hall. I couldn't imagine somebody that together ever cheating on his wife before she died – not that he couldn't cheat, I just couldn't imagine he would. I chose to never make that possibility part of my fantasy. The few times that I had spoken to him, he'd been nothing less than a gentleman, not even a hint of flirtation, but, of course, we had only spoken in passing. My intercom rang, reeling me back in from my daydream. I smiled to myself as my secretary spoke.

"Vada, I have a call for you. It's Mr. Townes. Would you like for me to put him through?"

Involuntarily, I rolled my eyes. "Yes, thank you, Carolyn."

"Hey, baby, we still on for this evening?"

"Of course we are, unless you're calling to tell me that you can't make it."

"V, why you got to go there? So every now and then I have to cancel a date, that doesn't mean I don't want to be with you. You know I miss you when I'm not with you, girl, but I have a business to run. Some days I'm just not able to get away. That's just part of who I am – part of the package."

"I know. So, what's up?"

"Just called to make sure things were still on for tonight and to see if you wanted me to bring anything?"

"Excuse me? Who is this? Well, I'm feeling really special right now. What did I do to deserve this?"

"Ha, ha…V, you're funny – you know that? I'm sure there are plenty of women who wouldn't mind me showing up empty-handed…"

As he was talking, I looked up as Mr. Vishmell and a colleague sauntered passed my open door. He casually glanced in. I gave him an unassuming, closed lip smile. He cordially returned the gesture.

William was still talking. "…but you know I love you. V, are you still there?"

"Sorry, I was distracted for a minute. What'd you say?"

"I said I love you, girl. Come on now."

"Oh…I love you too, William. I need to get some work done. I'll see you tonight…sevenish, okay?"

"Okay, but you never said whether or not you wanted me to bring anything."

"If you show up, baby, that'll be enough." I silently sighed and rolled my eyes.

"Don't be trying to make a brotha feel bad."

"I apologize. Surprise me."

After hanging up the phone, I stared at the door hoping Mr. Vishmell would pass by just one more time. Seeing him again would guarantee a permanent smile on my face for the remainder of the day.

———

As I drove home I thought about something William said during our earlier conversation. He said he was sure there were plenty of women who wouldn't mind him showing up empty-handed. As Dee often said, he is a pretty boy. So, I didn't need him telling me other women were interested in him. I realized he couldn't own a successful restaurant and be in the public eye, like he is, without being approached by women. Maybe he was just exercising his ego, as he so often does; I don't know. I'd never had a reason before now to doubt his faithfulness. I smiled when I considered how happy Dee would be if I broke up with him. What's really funny is how William doesn't pay any attention to what she thinks about him, even though he's well aware of it. He believes she might be attracted to him, but he said he would 'never' consider hitting on a friend of mine, even if he and I broke up. Said that would just be foul. Oh, well. *Tonight I'll ask him what he meant when he made that sarcastic comment about other women.*

————

After dinner, William and I settled in the family room. I watched him as he walked over to the couch where I was sitting. With my head slightly tilted, I meditatively examined him and was reminded of what caught my eye the first time I saw him: honey colored skin, wavy, black hair, light brown eyes and his muscles, which seemed to have a life of their own.

He sat down, almost on my lap. "What'cha thinkin' about, girl?"

"You…"

He pulled me into his chest as he spoke. "What about me?"

"William, you know what? You're a good looking man. I had forgotten how good looking until tonight. You must get hit on all the time, by women and men."

"Baby, I don't straddle the fence. I'm all man."

I laughed. "I know; that was a joke. I was thinking about what you said earlier today, though."

"What was that?"

"You said something about other women being glad to have you. Were you trying to tell me something? You and I have never had sex, but I don't really know…and to be honest with you, have never really thought about it until today, if you're having sex with anybody else, I mean."

"Where is this coming from? You must have talked with Dee before I got here?"

"No, this is not a Dee thing. This is a 'you and me thing.'"

"V, baby, I love you. You said you wanted to wait until we were married and I like that. I feel like I have a prize. Everybody doesn't get the opportunity or the privilege to experience purity. It's a beautiful thing."

"Okay, we know I'm a virgin, but have you been with any other women since we've been together? You know I don't expect you to say that you haven't been with anybody in all the years that we've known each other."

William nodded his head. "I see. I know where this is coming from – your situation with your pops!"

"Uh, uh…"

"Yeah, that's what this is. You think because your pops is kicking it with another woman that 'all' men must be doing it. I'm not your pops, baby. Don't put me in that category."

I sat up and pulled away from him, to look at him face-to-face. "What category is that?"

William reached out and hugged me back to his

chest. "Baby, the last thing I want to do is talk about your pops and his problems. I apologize. I was out of line. I know that's a sore spot right now. So, I don't want to go there. Even though it's your parents' problem, I'm going to continue to be patient with you. One of these days you'll see that this is about your folks, not you. But like I said, it has nothing to do with you, me, or us."

I pulled away from him again and sat up. "What do you mean you've been patient with me? You're my man; you're supposed to support and comfort me when it's necessary. And it is my problem. I'm not going to apologize for how I feel about what's going on with my parents right now."

"V, look, you're a grown woman. You need to get over it. Seems like your mom is doing fine…and she slept with him for forty years. Let them handle their own problems. Be for real now. You're not representing either one of them in court. And I'm sure there's more to the story than you're aware of…"

I had never been as angry with William as I was at this moment. "So, what I'm hearing is that you're unwilling to support me through this?"

"I'll do whatever it takes to comfort you: rub your back, give you massages, make love to you…but, see, we don't do the sex thing."

"What does that have to do with you supporting me in something that's important to me?"

William rubbed his head, sighed heavily, and stood up. "You know what? It's time for me to leave. I'm not going to sit here and argue with you about this. The

34

conversation is just going from one thing to the next and you're not making any sense."

I looked up at him, but refused to stand. "I tell you what, if you walk out that door you're telling me that you cannot and will not be there for me when I need you. And if you can't deal with this, then what can you deal with?"

Before responding he gave me an unyielding glare. "I'm going to say good night. You might want to think about what you're saying."

I finally stood to my feet. "Oh, I might want to think about what I'm saying? I meant what I said. Maybe you should reconsider walking out that door. And you know what? You never answered my original question."

"Good night, V."

"William?"

"Good night, V…"

———

April 26, 2012

It's been about a month since the last time I talked with William. I don't know who's more stubborn, him or me. But I do know this…I'm not going to call him! I don't care how many messages he leaves. I still can't believe he got up and walked out while we were talking. Dee is the happiest that I've seen her in years. She feels like this more than makes up for my dad's indiscretions. She's crazy. Maybe one day she'll tell me why she hates William "sooo" much.

Been over a month since my Dad left too. Hadn't talked to him at all before yesterday. Didn't have anything that I wanted to say to him. He called me at work and asked if we could meet for lunch on Saturday. I agreed to meet him. Though, I'm still pretty disgusted and disappointed by the whole thing. First time in my life that I've ever felt this way about him. Crazy thing is, I'm feeling so many things that I'm still not sure what I'm feeling. Talked with Mom this morning. She seems to be doing just fine…

I HAVE GOT TO GET A LIFE!!!!

THANKFUL FOR: a friend like Dee and seeing my dad on Saturday

Chapter 6

I grimaced at the idea of getting up at 6 o'clock in the morning on a Saturday to go to the gym. Who, other than JD and Greg, would go workout this early? They should be home with their wives. If they weren't my favorite cousins I wouldn't have dreamed of getting out of my bed to leave the house this early on the weekend.

As I parked my car I could see them standing in the lobby talking with two women. By the look of the workout ensembles that the two women were wearing, they had obviously come to the gym to do more than workout. Okay, so I'm back at square one. Do all men cheat? I quickly parked my car, so I could run in and block.

As I trotted across the parking lot, I tried to think of something witty to say: *Good morning boys, did your wives start their workouts without you; or, maybe, did you leave the kids home this morning; or, better yet, it's so sweet to see y'all talking with women for a change.* I laughed out loud at my last thought. They would kill me if I said that though.

As I opened the door to the lobby, Greg was the first one to see me, but before he could say anything I spoke up. "Hey guys! I ran into your wives in the parking lot. They should be in here in a minute."

JD looked at me as if to say that ain't even cool. Greg cut his eyes at me too. My plan worked because the chicks walked away after telling the guys they'd see them another time. Even after hearing they were married, they still might see them later? *What's wrong with women who make it easy for men to cheat?*

The workout with JD and Greg was great, but I ended up leaving early after getting pissed off because neither one of them could empathize with what I was going through. It was the first time in my life that we didn't see eye to eye on something. I guess it was a male thing. Both of them seemed to take their uncle's side – understanding where he was coming from – the flesh is weak and sometimes it succumbs to carnal desires. In the short time since my father had left, I had managed to create a riff in three of the most significant male relationships I had.

As I closed the door to my car I spoke out loud: "I'll be glad when this storm passes."

———

Little did I know how interesting lunch with my dad would be; we had agreed to meet at our favorite restaurant, JoJo's. The anxiety that I was experiencing was comparable to how I felt when I went out on a blind date before William and I met. The hostess escorted me to the patio. As I slowly worked my way to his table, I thought about our last conversation and tried to recall all of the questions I had rehearsed in the car on my ride to the restaurant. My mind went blank as I took what felt like a death march to meet a man that I had held in high esteem my entire life.

As I stepped onto the patio I recognized my father

from the back. I smiled to myself, but quickly realized he wasn't alone. There was a small child with him…a little girl. I stopped for a second to assess the situation. *Surely…nah, uh, uh…she can't belong to my dad? My dad…my dad has a little girl?* I quickly regained my composure, but I could feel myself getting angry.

"Hi, Daddy…," I tried to sound normal, but my voice was flat and lifeless.

He stopped what he was doing. Turning towards the sound of my voice, he stood up to give me a familiar hug.

"VJ, I'm so glad you came. I've missed you." He waived his hand over my chair as he pulled it from the table. "Here, baby. Sit here."

I sat down with an uncontrollable furrow in my brow as I looked at him, and then quickly glanced at the smiling, neatly dressed little girl that sat across from me. She was oblivious to the fact that her presence made me uneasy. My dad's words brought me back to the present.

"Princess, this is your big sister."

I looked at him and thought: *Did he just call her princess? I used to be his princess.* I continued to look at the little girl, and though the child spoke, I didn't hear a word she was saying.

Daddy continued with his awkward introduction. "VJ, this is your little sister, Monyet."

My mind raced. *Okay, he just said this innocent, unassuming, little girl dressed in turquoise and white was my little sister. This divorce has gone from bad to worse. Not fair! Not fair! I wasn't prepared to meet a love child. Who is this man sitting at the table, Monyet's daddy?* We hadn't even ordered yet and I was ready to leave.

I watched the innocent little by-stander in turquoise and white before turning my attention to my dad.

Seething, but as calmly as possible, I asked, "How could you do this to me? You didn't think the divorce was enough? I can't believe that you thought I would be prepared for something like this. Do you even know me anymore?"

"Vada Jade, this isn't about you."

"Well, then, if it's not about me, why does this hurt so much? You seem to have all of the answers these days, answer that." My lips were drawn tight across my face as I challenged him with my eyes.

He had taught me well. Daddy wanted to keep me from being taking advantage of as I grew up. He knew the world could be cruel to a woman, especially a black woman. He wanted me to be prepared to stand tall and face whatever obstacles lie ahead of me. He now found himself my biggest obstacle yet. I was sitting as his judge and jury…and he was well aware that no argument he presented would be enough to exonerate him in my eyes, not today anyway. His moral infraction was merely a selfish desire: a selfish desire to feel younger, to recapture his youth. He was right about one thing, though; it had nothing to do with me…or my mother, for that matter. He also had to know, deep down in his heart, that if he truly loved us more than he loved himself he would never have left. Now he's in a situation that he can't back out of. He has fathered this beautiful, little girl outside of his marriage.

In between making the waiter uncomfortable and ordering our meal, we sat at the table and looked at each other from time to time, before anything else was said.

When I finally opened my mouth to speak, my words were sharp and direct. "How could you do this to us, Daddy? How could you leave like this, like we're nothing, like we've never meant anything to you? How could you do this to Mom? And then you add insult to injury by inviting me to have lunch with you and your illegitimate child."

I couldn't imagine that there was anything he could say that would make me feel better, but that didn't stop him from trying.

"I didn't think that I was doing anything 'to' your mother, as much as I was doing something 'for' myself. All my life I said I would never be like my father. When I was a boy I saw him cheat on your grandmother. For goodness sakes, your granddad used to actually introduce me to his women friends. I promised myself that I would always love my wife and my children more than that, that I would respect them more than that. One day I woke up and, uh, you were grown, independent, and self-sufficient. A certain need wasn't there anymore. Your mother and I were like furniture to each other. So, I just moved on. Your mother seemed to be going on with her life, too. She went back to school and got her Ph.D. I don't know, I just moved on to where I felt needed. And before I knew it, I had become my father."

I felt the furrow deepen in my forehead. "What do you mean you went where you felt needed? I've always needed you. What makes you think that I don't need you now?"

I grabbed my napkin from my lap and dabbed at the corners of my eyes. I had hoped I wouldn't cry. I could forget about that now.

"When you were a little girl you helped me with everything. Do you remember: When you were about seven or eight years old we were painting the deck and you turned and looked at me and said, 'Daddy, look at me. I can paint by myself. I'm a big girl now!' I looked at you and said, 'Yeah, you're Daddy's big girl.' Do you remember that? I do. From that day on it seemed like you grew up faster and faster. The next thing I knew you were graduating from high school, then college, then you were moving out of the house…then law school. Soon after that you purchased your own home. I just didn't feel like you needed me anymore. I knew that it would only be a matter of time before you met the man that you were going to marry and he would finally replace me in your life. Your mother, well, she had gone back to school and gotten her Ph.D. She was traveling all of the time. She just didn't seem to need me the way she did when we first got married." He paused and stared at me. "I felt like I should move on because somebody somewhere did need me. So, here I am…and here's Monyet." He turned and gave Monyet a half smile as he stroked her hair.

Chuckling, mostly to myself, I looked down at my

hands. I couldn't believe this was the same man that raised me and helped me to become the person that I am. I had no appetite…I felt weak and defeated, and, frankly, I was sick to my stomach. I looked back up at him and, as best I could, I wanted to tell him what I was feeling, even though I felt woefully ill-prepared to do so.

"Dad, you're certainly entitled to have your own feelings, but I feel like my children have lost out on something special; something that they will never have an opportunity to experience because the entire scene of our lives have changed. I always imagined that I'd bring my children back home to visit their grandparents. Now when I do that, I'll have to take them to visit their grandmother in one house and their grandfather in another…with his new family. It just doesn't seem right. I believe that there are always only two real choices in life…the right one or the wrong one. This time you chose wrong, without considering how that choice would affect anyone else in your life, but, like I said, you're certainly entitled to making your own choices."

Reaching across the table, Daddy grabbed my hand and held it. "VJ, I'm not going to tell you that you're wrong to feel what you feel, but regarding your children...that's a little while coming. We'll cross that bridge when we get to it."

…and so went lunch with my dad and his daughter, my little sister, his new princess, Monyet.

———

April 28, 2012

My dad has a daughter named Monyet: a pretty name for a pretty little girl that should really be my daughter, his granddaughter. He seemed happy and the little girl basked in his love…simply because she was there with him. Her daddy…

It takes a great deal of work, dedication, and love to make a happy family and so little to destroy it. I pose a question: If the king abdicates his throne and becomes a commoner, what becomes of the queen and the princess?

THANKFUL FOR: life, breath, and cleansing tears

Chapter 7

I can't believe I'm running late for work. This never happens. This is what I get for hanging out with Dee, trying to act like we're 20 years old again. As soon as I get to work I'm going to call her and tell her about herself.

And so began my day. The last day of the weekend, the day before a workday and Dee and I had decided – well, Dee decided I needed to get out of the house and do something. She asked her dad to keep Quincy for the day, so I had no idea what I was in for. We began the day by working out at the gym. After working out we sat in the sauna and talked for about 20 minutes. I had sufficiently worked out the stress from the previous day's lunch with my dad, so I was now ready to share the highlights with Dee.

"Did I tell you I was having lunch with my dad yesterday?"

Dee was lying on the bench across from me with her arm across her forehead. "I'm sure you probably did. How'd it go?"

"I guess it went okay. We ate and talked. There was more talking than eating, though. He looked good. Monyet was gorgeous."

Dee sat up and gave me her full attention. "Monyet? Daddy Bassett had the nerve to bring his jump-off to lunch? Girl, that's scandalous. How'd that work for you?"

I wiped a little sweat from my forehead. "It's not what you think. Monyet is his little girl."

Dumbfounded, Dee jumped to her feet and walked towards me. "What? What? Unbelievable! Okay, I am convinced that your daddy has lost his mind. I mean really, I wonder what he could have been thinking. How old is this child?" Dee now stood in front of me with her hands on her hips.

Dee's towel had fallen off of her head, so her hair was disheveled and wild.

"You need to get from in front of me with your hands on your slight hips and go back over there and sit down."

She grabbed her towel up off the floor and sat back down, poised to hear more.

"Well, I would say Monyet is about two or three years old…and she's absolutely adorable." My mind wandered back to the happy, little girl in turquoise and white, adoringly smiling at her dad, our dad, like he was the king of the world – just like I used to look at him. I thought about how one day he would begin to teach that little girl the same things he taught me: that she is as beautiful as she is intelligent. How she would grow up to appreciate the strength and character that she wasn't even aware that he was molding in her. I smiled when I considered how that little girl would one day see her relationship with her daddy as special – just like I used to.

"Where are you, baby? Come back, finish telling me what happened."

I looked over at Dee and smiled. Even though I could

feel the sting of tears in my eyes, I laughed out loud. "I'm here, just thinking about things."

"Like what?"

"How fortunate Monyet is to have such a wonderfully attentive daddy."

After the sauna we showered and went to brunch. Dee decided we should talk a little more about how I really felt about my most recent revelation. There was no drama to share; I was disappointed, yet surprisingly calm. I couldn't even explain it at the time. I thought maybe I was either in denial or experiencing some type of mild break down. After brunch we went to a matinee, and then walked through the mall. Even though I was ready to call it a day, Dee insisted 5 o'clock was too early to go home. So, we left the mall and drove uptown to one of my favorite spots, Baile Salamandra, an upscale Latino dance club. Dee's answer to everything was men, music, and dancing. In her words, "What better way to get over a bad day than to dance with some handsome men?"

Since salsa dancing was my thing, Dee knew it would help sidestep the possibility of me falling into an emotional slump. What can I say? She's my girl.

So, now it's 8:40 a.m. on Monday and I find myself running through the parking deck. When I woke up and realized I had overslept, I soon thereafter remembered I had a 9:00 a.m. meeting – *Of all days to have a meeting, after a night of margaritas and salsa dancing until one in the morning.* As I approached the closing elevator doors, I dropped my purse. *Shoot, now I'm really going to be late. It'll probably take forever before another elevator arrives.* As I picked my purse up from the marble floor, I glanced up to find a hand holding the doors open. As I stood up, I realized the hand belonged to Hayes Foreman Vishmell.

Hoping I didn't look too sweaty and mussy from running across the parking deck, I stammered, "Good morning. Thank you for being so kind."

He smiled. "Good morning. It's my pleasure. Do you need help with anything?"

"No, I'm fine, thank you." I stepped into the waiting elevator.

For what seemed like minutes, but what was surely only seconds, we stood there uncomfortably silent. Apparently, neither of us knew what to say next. I looked at our reflections in the mirrored doors. Actually, I gazed at his reflection. I was lost in thought about how good he looked in his suit when he finally spoke again.

"Please, excuse my manners." He extended his hand. "My name is Hayes…"

"…Vishmell. I know. I'm VJ…"

"…Bassett. I know."

If there was any question as to whether or not he really knew who I was, his eyes assured me, he knew.

We both laughed a very comfortable and familiar laugh, which seemed to ease our apprehension. I felt myself blushing. Something I hadn't done in years.

"It's a pleasure to meet you, Mr. Vishmell."

"Please, call me Hayes."

I smiled.

"This might sound a little forward, but are you free for dinner …tonight."

I cocked my head to one side and looked at him. "Do you always hold elevator doors open for women and then ask them out?"

He laughed a hearty, guttural laugh. "No, I don't always make special effort to hold elevator doors open for beautiful women and then ask them out."

"Well, then I'm extremely flattered. What if we do lunch instead? Dinner seems so serious. I mean, really, all you did was hold the elevator door open for me."

"Lunch it is. I have a meeting with a client at10:30, so I'll call you as soon as I finish."

We stepped off of the elevator together. I wondered if he was thinking the same thing I was thinking. *What just happened in that elevator?* I couldn't get in my office fast enough…to call Dee.

———

I was totally distracted during my 9 o'clock meeting. As soon as it ended I shook hands with my perspective clients and all but ran to my office. 10:30 came and went. 11 o'clock came and went. Noon came and went. No Hayes. I wondered if I should call him, maybe he forgot. At 1:30 my phone rang. I smiled and cleared my throat in an attempt to avoid sounding anxious.

After a deep breath I spoke. "VJ Bassett."

"I know who I'm calling. How was lunch? Tell me what's really going on with that chocolate cowboy."

It was just Dee.

"You know you're a fool, right?"

"Sure do, now tell me about lunch."

"Unfortunately, there's nothing to tell. We never made it. I haven't heard from him since this morning."

"What, he stood you up?"

"I don't think it's anything like that." I paused.

"What? VJ…"

"Oh, let me call you back. My other line is ringing. It's him."

"Call me right back, as soon as you hang up."

"Hello, this is VJ."

"This is Hayes. VJ, I sincerely apologize. My meeting went much longer than I anticipated. It continued right through lunch. I don't know why, but I didn't feel comfortable asking my secretary to call you."

A yielding smile spread across my face. "I understand. I've attended a meeting or two like that myself. All is forgiven."

"Good. It would be an honor and a pleasure if you would allow me to make this up to you with dinner…tonight."

"If I didn't know any better, I'd think this was your plan all along."

"No diabolical plans, Ms. Bassett. You have my word."

"Okay, if you say so. Where and what time should we meet?"

"If it's okay, I'd like to come by your office when I finish and perhaps we can ride to the restaurant together?"

"I was thinking we'd meet at the restaurant. That way we don't have to come back by the office to pick up my car. Six o'clock works for me, how about for you?"

"You present a sound argument, Counselor. I'll meet you at Mozzo's at 6 o'clock and not a minute later. You have my word."

"Mozzo's it is. I'll see you there."

Hayes had unknowingly picked one of my favorite restaurants. It was only about 15 minutes away from the office, so my plan was to finish what I was doing, run by the ladies room to freshen up, and stop by Dee's office on my way out. Forget calling her, I wanted to make sure I looked totally put together when I arrived for dinner. I couldn't believe how nervous I was. You would think we were going out on a date or something. I stopped for a minute. *Wow, this is the first day in a long time that I didn't spend the entire day thinking about my mom and dad...or William.* I smiled and nodded my head in approval.

The healing had begun.

———

After getting the once over by Dee, I found myself practically running to my car. This was the second time in one day that I had felt that little girlish anticipation. Surely I was over thinking things, but it wasn't even like I had considered anything about Hayes, other than the fact that he was an extremely handsome man and I was excited by the mere sight of him. Maybe it was because he seemed to be so different than William or any of the other men who had ever approached me. I really needed to stop tripping, and I knew it. It's just dinner with a colleague. I've done this a million times before.

"When Hayes arrived at the restaurant I was sitting at the bar. I didn't want to appear too anxious, even though I was having a difficult time relaxing.

"VJ, I hope I didn't keep you waiting long?"

"Not at all, I've only been here long enough to sit down."

"Have you gotten us a table yet?"

"No, I thought I should wait for you to arrive. You know, just in case." I smiled and raised my eyebrows.

Hayes nodded. "Touché, I deserve that. I'll ask the hostess to get us a table."

I had gotten so use to William dropping me off at the door to get a table while he parked the car that it was actually very refreshing to have Hayes get a table for us.

Mozzo's has a very warm and comfortable, eclectic atmosphere. You name it, they probably serve it. It's the first and only place where I have ever had grilled Asian barbecue duck breast. The building itself was two stories high and had a floor to ceiling storefront window. If you wanted to be cozier, there were the curtained booths on both the first and second floor, as well as a bar area that looked like a nice comfy living room. The walls of the restaurant were beautiful red suede and the artwork and mirrors were some of the most interesting pieces I'd ever seen. We were led to a very cozy curtained booth on the second floor.

Hayes held the curtain open for me. I thanked him

and sat down. *Whoa, this feels like a doggone date.* I couldn't remember the last time William had even held the chair for me or if he had ever done it, now that I thought about it. I intently watched Hayes as he sat down. I couldn't believe I was sitting here with the man that I stare at all the time. *What the heck is this about?* I smiled and he smiled back. His smile actually seemed to calm me down.

"So, VJ, have you ever been to Mozzo's before?"

"When you suggested coming here I thought it was pretty ironic that you would choose it because it's actually one of my favorite places."

"Good, I'm glad. That's the least I could do after standing you up for lunch. I want to apologize again for that. It was the strangest thing. I wanted to take a break and call you, and then I thought I should have my secretary do it, but I just didn't feel comfortable asking her to make the call."

I shrugged my shoulders. "Why was that?"

The waiter came back and asked if we were ready to order. I wasn't, but Hayes asked if it was okay if he ordered us some appetizers and a bottle of wine.

After the waiter walked away, Hayes finally responded. "I really don't know. I can't say that I was embarrassed. It was more like I was just bashful about letting her know that you and I had lunch plans. I'm telling you, it was just strange."

"That is strange. I'm a colleague. Why would she have a problem with us going to lunch? Is she good friends with your wife?" I thought it was pretty clever

53

the way I was able to slip that question in there. I knew he was a widower, but I didn't know how to bring it up.

"Well, Helen has been my secretary for years. So, she knows me better than most people. I guess I just didn't want her in my business. If I had mentioned that I was going to lunch with you she would have had some commentary about it. And for the record, she was very good friends with my wife. I'm a widower."

For some reason, actually hearing him say the words out loud totally overshadowed any question I might have had about Helen having something to say about us going out to lunch.

"I'm so sorry. Was she ill?"

The waiter returned with the wine and poured a glass for each of us. I needed it, quickly. I had opened my mouth and inserted my foot. We ordered our dinner and returned to our conversation before the curtain could close behind the waiter as he turned to walk away.

"About my wife, yes and no, it's been four years. Sometimes it seems like it was just yesterday and other times it feels like she's been gone forever."

"If you don't mind me asking, what happened?"

"Cancer…"

He looked like his mind wandered away when he said the "C" word. I wanted to get up and hug him, but, somehow, that just didn't seem to be appropriate. So, instead, I reached across the table and gently put my hand on top of his and squeezed.

"We don't have to talk about it if it's uncomfortable for you."

"It's okay. We also don't want this to be a depressing dinner."

I smiled. "I agree."

We both looked at my hand, which was still resting on his. I thought it better to use that hand to now lift another glass of wine to my lips.

"So, VJ, tell me about yourself? Are you married?"

"No, I can't say that I've had that pleasure yet, but hopefully one day."

"I don't think you'll have a problem with that. You're beautiful and intelligent, probably very outgoing, as well. Some man is going to be very fortunate. You probably have men knocking your door down."

"Well, thank you, Mr. Vishmell."

"Hayes...," he corrected me.

"Hayes," I repeated after him. "I actually just ended a relationship. We'd been together for almost three years." I paused for a second. "Yeah, it was just about three years."

"...and he never asked you to marry him?"

"No, but I think part of that was me; I'm not quite ready to be married."

"Maybe you just weren't ready to marry him."

"Maybe," I nodded.

He nodded his head too. "Okay..."

"Do you have any children?"

"Yes, and two grandchildren," Hayes responded proudly.

"You have grandchildren?"

"Two, Lydia and Owen; Lydia's three years old and

Owen is six months."

"They're both still fun ages. Your wife never got a chance to see either of them. That's too bad."

"Unfortunately, no, she didn't. My daughter had just found out she was pregnant when my wife received her diagnosis."

Our conversation continued to flow very comfortably as our food was served. It didn't even seem to matter anymore that we talked about his wife. At some point I even wished I could have met her. *What kind of woman was she to be so fortunate as to have a man like this? And* w*hat kind of man is he, really?*

"So, you have grandchildren. That means you have at least the one daughter?"

Hayes looked almost uncomfortable responding. "I have three children, a daughter and two sons. Both grandchildren belong to my daughter. She's the oldest. She's 31 and the boys are 28 and 29."

I unconsciously responded with just a sound. "Humph…"

"What was that for?"

"Your daughter isn't that much younger than me. Well, for that matter, neither are your sons."

"I hope that's not a problem?"

I watched him as he continued to eat. "Why would that be a problem?"

"…because I'd like to take you out again." The look on his face took control of my heart.

"Oh …oh, okay."

He continued, as if he hadn't just made a

groundbreaking statement. "We've spent so much time talking about me. I really would like to get to know you better…away from the office, if you don't mind."

———

April 30, 2012

Dinner with Hayes earlier tonight was wonderful. We closed the place down. I like him. I like him a lot…Hayes Vishmell. Mr. Vishmell is a refreshing change from William Morris Townes, III. Good! I called Dee on the way home to tell her about dinner. She must have been sitting on the phone because it rang exactly one half rings before she answered. She was full of questions. She started off by asking me how dinner was. She also wanted to know if he was really all that. I had to laugh…it was just dinner, but my first impression is that he is "all that." One of the best dinners I've ever had – because of the company – but, I'm making myself keep in mind that it was still just dinner. I'm so sleepy I'm feeling punch drunk. I'm going to bed now. I like him…I really like that Hayes Vishmell.

THANKFUL FOR: not being mad at men anymore… and for getting over William

Chapter 8

May 9, 2012

Hayes and I have dinner plans for tomorrow evening. He wants to cook for me. He claims he's a pretty good cook. I guess we'll see about that. This last week we've had lunch together once and we've met for dinner once. We made plans to catch a movie over the weekend or go to the park, depending on the weather. Work has taken on a different meaning. I've never hated going, but it's been much more pleasurable this week. Hayes has taken to stopping at my office door…just to say hi. I just want to look at him. He fills me with smiles. Of course, it's early yet, so I'm not quite sure where this is going, but it's really nice…and different with him.

Dee and I are going out for dinner tonight. She wants to school me on how to act when I go to Haye's house tomorrow night. She thinks, because I didn't date much before William, that I'm clueless and, on the other hand, having dated considerably more than me, she claims to know the ins and outs of dating an older man. She has assured me that dating Hayes is going to be nothing like dating William. According to her, older men are more refined, if they're nice guys, but they can be just as trifling as the younger guys, who think they know what's going on, but instead are learning as they go along…unless they have really good mamas. Even though I sometimes think Dee is ridiculous, I can't write enough about seeing a very pleasant difference between William and Hayes. William made me happy, but he never made me feel like I was smiling on the inside. Surprisingly, sex has not entered into any of the conversations with Hayes, but of course it's only been a week. I guess I better make it a point to bring it up tomorrow night, so that Hayes doesn't have any expectations.

THANKFUL FOR: waking up this morning, good health, good job, and good friends

---

I followed Dee home, so I could drop my car off. We ran in to speak to her dad and to give Quincy a quick hug.

As we pulled out of the driveway Dee turned and looked at me. "So, what does all of this feel like?"

"What do you mean?"

"How do you feel? I only ask because you're looking radiant these days."

I looked at her and rolled my eyes. "What?"

"No, really; you are absolutely glowing."

"Psss…you're crazy. Since you know so much, you tell me why I'm looking so radiant because I didn't realize I was."

"Girl, please. Everybody else can see it too. I don't know why you can't."

"Everybody like who? Nobody has said a word to me about anything."

"Well, I can assure you, you are the talk of the office. I'm happy for you because I haven't seen you this happy in years. I think Hayes Vishmell is the best thing to happen to you since...since we graduated from law school and partied like it was 1999. Seriously, though, VJ, you look like you've gone through some kind of metamorphosis and people are talking. It doesn't help that a few people have seen you and Hayes out together. I heard some of the older chicks around the office trippin'."

I had to interrupt Dee because I hadn't heard or seen anything to indicate anybody even knew that I was going out with him.

"Trippin' about what? So we've been out to eat a few times. What's the big deal?"

"Look, you know just as well I do that Hayes is a great catch and that women around that office, old and young, fall to the floor like he's some kind of superstar when he walks through the room. I heard he dated a couple of women in the office. Well, he went out with them, but he ended the relationships very quickly, for whatever reason. To be honest with you, I don't think he has seriously dated anyone since his wife died. I think he's gone out on a couple of dates and the women blew things out of proportion because they were out with him, and the brother just didn't ask them out again. VJ, the man has it going on and it is impossible to deny that."

"Okay, from outward appearances, he does seem to have his stuff in order..."

"....uh, huh, and..."

"He has it going on!" I laughed. "Okay, is that what you want to hear?"

Dee sat quietly before responding. "And…"

"…and I don't really have a word to describe how he makes me feel. The closest I can come to describing it is that he makes me feel like I'm smiling on the inside. Like I said, we've only gone out a few times."

"Uh, huh…lunch and dinner, but who's counting. And trust me, friend, you're not just smiling on the inside."

"Anyway, with your crazy self, you exaggerate. I would say things seem promising with him though."

"That's because he's so pretty, a rugged kind of pretty, like a cowboy."

"As I was saying, I know it's only been a week, but he seems like the kind of guy that would stand beside me or behind me, if you will, and support whatever endeavor I chose to involve myself in. I feel like anything is possible with him. Not to mention, he makes me feel maternal. Isn't 'that' crazy?"

As Dee sat back gazing at me, she became unusually quiet. I even thought I saw tears in her eyes. "All jokes aside, that was really beautiful. I hope the brother is real. I hope he's everything that you think he is, and more. You're my best friend and I love you just as much, if not more than I love my flesh and blood sister. I want to always know that you're happy…always. Life ain't really been too bad for either one of us, discounting my mother's death, the unfortunate demise of my marriage, and your parent's recent separation, but I just think you deserve to find that kind of happiness after wasting all of those years with William. What you said about smiling on the inside, that's what I want again. There was a time when I actually had that with Quincy's father. So, I sort of know how you feel. Anyway…I'm happy for you. And what's this maternal feeling that you're talking about? It's only been a week, so don't get too caught up in all of the feelings and miss the man."

The conversation was getting a little heavy for me, so I thought I better lighten things up a bit. I knew Dee frequently put on a tough, take no mess persona, but behind the hard veneer she still loved Quincy, Jr., her son's father. I always thought all of Dee's dating was to distract her from how she really felt after her divorce.

"Thank you for all of that, but I'm completely aware of the fact that I just officially met the man. So, if I were you, I wouldn't be looking for a maid of honor dress or for an 'I'm a great auntie' T-shirt any time soon. Know what I mean?"

Dee gave me a sly smile. "Okay, if you say so. Where are we going anyway?"

"You know that little bistro on River's Edge? I was thinking we could go there."

"That's just as good as any place else. If I recall correctly, they have a really good bar and some cute bartenders."

"They have really good food too, Dee."

"Okay, whatever."

———

After turning the car over to the valet we walked into the restaurant. As we watched the hostess add our names to the waiting list for a table, I looked to my right and saw William at a table eating with a very buxomly woman.

I nudged Dee. "Don't make a scene, and try not to be obvious, but look over to your right."

Dee looked up and very discreetly glanced over her right shoulder. "I know that ain't William Townes over there feeding that hoochie?"

"Why does she have to be a hoochie, Dee? So what if he's feeding her."

"So, you're telling me that doesn't bother you...not even a little bit? He probably has been seeing her for some time. Don't you think?"

"Why would you say that? The same could be said about me and Hayes."

"Honey, I doubt very seriously that anybody could walk up on you and Hayes anytime soon and catch y'all feeding each other in public. If I walked into his house tomorrow night while y'all were having dinner, I bet I wouldn't catch y'all feeding each other then either. Stop trippin'."

As we sat down to wait for our table, I began to recall an incident from a while ago: *One night I showed up unannounced at William's restaurant right before closing. I thought I would surprise him and have a late dinner with him. As I think back on it now, the woman he's sitting at the table with is looking more and more familiar to me. Everyone had left the restaurant, except for the staff and a woman sitting alone at a table close to the back of the room. I had walked in from the foyer after speaking to the maitre d' and asking him where I could find Mr. Townes. He had suggested checking the office or the kitchen. As I walked toward the kitchen, to check there first, William stepped through the door. Without looking in my direction, he walked toward the table where the woman was sitting. I stopped and watched him because the woman's face lit up as he approached her. He extended both of his hands and grabbed her hands as he kissed her on the cheek. I couldn't hear what either one of them was saying. So, at the time, I took it all in stride. To me, the initial impression was that she was one of William's many restaurant groupies and that she had hung around till closing. As I approached them I called out his name.*

Now that I think back on it, he did look a little startled when he turned and realized it was me. He quickly excused himself from the table and walked towards me. We were never ones for public displays of affection, so it didn't seem peculiar when he hugged me and ushered me off to his office.

I wonder why I never thought about that incident before now. How he kissed me on my forehead before he left me in his office for over 15 minutes, or how he minimized the significance of what I also witnessed that night after leaving the office to find him: the long lingering hug he was giving the other woman, the woman who I now recognized as the same one sitting at the table with him.

Dee awoke me from my trance. "Are you okay? Our table is ready."

As we were escorted to our table, it became obvious that we were going to walk pass William.

Dee whispered to me, "You gonna say something to that knucklehead or can I?"

"Nah, girl, let me say something to him."

As we approached him from the back, he had just fed something to his friend and was now motioning to kiss her.

I stopped at his table and put my hand on his right shoulder. "William Morris Townes, III, how are you? I didn't think you were ever away from your own restaurant during the dinner crowd?"

He practically choked when he realized it was me.

Coughing, he grabbed his napkin and covered his mouth. "Oh…hey…uhm…V. Uh…yeah…Dee. V, look at you, you look good girl."

I gave him a closed lip smile and quickly glanced over at his dinner partner, who was leering at me. Not to worry, though, I was looking as good as I felt.

Dee's chimed in. "Who's your friend…William?" She rolled her eyes and neck as she looked the woman up and down.

"Yeah, I'm sorry, ladies this is Monique Tate. Monique this is Delaney Brown-Lofton….and VJ Bassett..." His voice trailed off just a little after he said my name.

Miss Thang was looking at him like, where do I know her from and I know you're going to tell me more than that about her.

Feeling we had sufficiently and successfully disrupted his dinner, we went on our way. I smiled at William as I bid him an apparently long overdue farewell, in more ways than one.

"Didn't mean to disturb you, just wanted to stop and say hello."

By now his lady friend was glaring at me, while William, for the first time that I could ever recall, sat there looking totally disheartened.

After we sat down, Dee and I ordered drinks, and then quickly thereafter ordered our meal.

Dee slightly leaned forward over the table. "Girl, how did that feel?"

I laughed. "Actually, it felt really good. The mind is amazing. It discards what you need to discard and recalls what you need to recall. While we were waiting on our table, I remembered where I've seen that Monique before."

"You've never said anything to me about it, I'm sure of that."

"Well, I saw her at William's restaurant about six months ago, or so. One night I went there right after closing to surprise him; Monique was sitting there waiting for him too."

"Get out of here! What happened?" Dee took a sip of her drink.

"Nothing – William took me in his office and obviously went back to get rid of her. I came out of the office just in time to see him hugging her goodbye. I asked him about it, but he told me it was nothing. He did what he always did; he talked himself right out of the situation. I wanted to believe him, so I did. I never asked him about her again, but there was another time I was driving down the street and I passed his car. I thought I saw a woman with him. And what made me just remember that is that I'm sure it was this same girl. That was, like, the end of last year, maybe. It's no tellin' how long he's been seeing her."

Dee was always looking for a reason to jump down William's throat. Now she had it. "I want to go over there and smack him right across his lying mouth. I never could stand him. I knew it. I knew it. You're taking this pretty calmly, though."

"What else is there to do? We haven't talked in over a month and I think I'm seeing somebody else anyway, right? What's done is done. I'm a little pissed, a little hurt, and a little disappointed, but good riddance."

"I'm glad that's your attitude. That's what makes me love you so much. You balance me out, girl. Because you know, if I was you and I caught my recently ex-boyfriend here with another chick, I think I would have turned this place out...and then fled the scene. I wouldn't care if I were dating a Hayes Vishmell or a Denzel Washington. It would have been on. And anyway, y'all just broke up. What's up with that nigga? Ooh, I can't stand him."

"Well, I'm glad it was me and not you." I laughed at her. "We both have reputations to maintain, and I don't think Allen, Vishmell, & Taylor would be too impressed with one or two of their junior attorneys getting arrested for simple battery and disorderly conduct."

We both sipped from our drinks and laughed.

The waiter arrived with our food, so that ended the conversation.

"Can I tell you something else?" Dee went on.

As I took a bite of food from my fork, I nodded my head. "Go ahead."

"I know you've always wondered why I didn't like William. So, I think I can tell you why now."

I stopped eating and looked at her. I had a foreboding feeling that my world was going to be rocked just a little more tonight.

"You know, I never liked the fact that you met him at a party that he had come to with another chick, but a little while after y'all start seeing each other…"

"What?" I put my fork down.

"A few weeks after y'all start seeing each other William tried me."

"What, exactly, do you mean by tried you?"

"He asked me if he could get with me. Shoot, the negro asked me if he could have sex with me."

"What? Why didn't…haven't you…told me about this before now? I don't understand. So, he asked you all of this and what? What, Dee?"

Dee sighed deeply. "I cussed his butt out and told him that I would kick his behind if he ever approached me like that again. I wanted him to break up with you and just get out of your life, but he refused to do that. I wasn't sure how you would take me telling you this guy you were digging so much was trying to kick it with your best girl. There were a few times I tried to talk to you about it, but you kept telling me that he had some things he needed to work out, and I didn't want you to think I was making up something just to break the two of you up. I knew if he was brazen enough to try to get with me then there was no telling who else he might kick it with."

"So, I've just been the fool for these last three years? You let me play the fool? What's that about? I love you and I can't imagine that I wouldn't have believed you."

"VJ, don't even go there with me. How many times have I told you other things about William and you went right back to him and asked him about it? And what happened? He did everything except for charm you out of your panties. You loved him and your parents seemed to love him because you loved him…even though I know they really never cared for him being with you. Am I wrong about any of that? Am I?"

I sat with my elbow on the table and my finger across my lips because I knew she was right. There were times when she told me things about William; about seeing him with other women; about seeing him somewhere where he wasn't supposed to be, and he was always able to convince me that it wasn't him or he had a change in plans, or whatever. I also knew that my mom and dad never really cared for us being together, but if I was happy they were happy with me. I consider myself intelligent, so how could I stay in a relationship with him as long as I did? And why wouldn't I pay attention to the signs or to what my people were telling me? How difficult would that have been? I guess the truth was I was never into William like I should have been. I was comfortable with seeing him occasionally because he made no real demands on me – no sexual demands, that is, especially since college, and no pressure to get married. Now I know for sure that it was easy for him to appear like he was respecting my wishes because he was spending his nights elsewhere. Big ole fool…I had been his fool for three years. I made it easy for him.

"I guess William thinks I'm just stupid. I agree, I was a little foolish, but I know I'm not stupid."

"You don't have to convince me of that, girl. I know you're not stupid. I agree that you've been a little foolish, but when it comes to men, who of us hasn't been at some time or another? I mean, really."

That's my girl, trying to keep me from beating myself up too much. I smiled and ate a little more of my meal.

"VJ, in spite of that good-for-nothing William, you're still glowing. I really admire how you handled him and that trick he's with – very dignified, very classy of you. There were so many other ways that situation could have played out. I bet she has probably spent the last 20 minutes trying to figure out who you are. He's going to call you. It might not be tonight, but he's going to call you. The fact that you look good and you didn't act a fool means something to him. As crazy as it is, men think that means they're still in good with you. They're so arrogant they make it about them. I'm sure he thinks you still want him too." Dee stopped to laugh. "He's going to call you and try you because you didn't sweat him and he's probably still thinking he has you fooled. Be ready for a good lie, though. He makes me sick. You know what? He's the past….and tomorrow there's Hayes Vishmell, right?"

With her barefoot, Dee kicked me under the table, and tilted her head in William's direction. I turned to watch him and his lady friend leaving the restaurant. As he motioned to touch her arm, she snatched away from him.

I smiled. "Good."

———

I was extremely impressed. Hayes proved to be a very good cook. After dinner he wouldn't allow me to help with the dishes, so I sat in the kitchen and watched him as he washed our dinner dishes. He was even more handsome without a suit on. I looked at him in his jeans and off-white, Ralph Lauren Polo shirt. The small diamond in his left ear sparkled every time the light hit it just right. Before tonight, I had never noticed that his ear was pierced.

"Dinner was very good. You cook and you wash dishes too. How many years have you been doing that, Mr. Vishmell?"

"I've washed dishes for at least 32 years now. When I first got married I began doing it just to spend a little more time with my wife. It became routine. If she arrived home first she cooked, and then I washed the dishes afterwards. If I got home first, I cooked and she washed the dishes. That allowed us to spend plenty of time together to talk about our day and anything else we wanted to talk about."

"That sounds really nice. You and your wife seemed to have had a very special relationship. Everybody isn't that fortunate."

"Well, it took a lot of work. I'm sure Celine thought I was trifling sometimes."

"I just can't imagine that, Hayes Vishmell trifling? Impossible."

"Not according to her. She kept me grounded, though; kept my feet on terra firma. She always reminded me that I was just another black man. Particularly when I began to think that I might just be a little bit more than average."

I laughed at the idea of him being arrogant. It didn't even seem possible. What kind of woman could humble a humble man even more?

"What was she like, your wife, I mean? She sounds like she was a beautiful person."

"Uh, where do I begin? Celine was about your height, but she was a little fairer skinned than you, long black hair, absolutely gorgeous. You would never have known it by talking with her, though. When I first met her she described herself as homey. She was actually Halle Berry beautiful. She worked out a lot because her secret desire was to be a dancer, and on the low she ate like a man. Let's see what else. She was very down to earth, extremely approachable, and easy to talk to. I believe she would have liked you…"

I interrupted. "Not under these circumstance, though, having dinner with her husband."

"No..." Hayes laughed. "If she thought a woman was flirting with me she'd eat her alive. Very secure in herself and very protective of what was hers. After our children were born she seemed to become even more protective. I really wish you could have met her." The tone of his voice changed. "Every day that I spent with her I became more and more captivated by her. Love doesn't even begin to describe how I felt about her."

As I watched Hayes washing the dishes, the Isley Brothers played in the background. He talked about this woman who held his attention for 32 years, who would have held it far into the future, had she not died. He seemed to soften as he described her. He leaned against the counter, his hands resting on the edge of the sink. His frame seemed to buckle just a hint, so I stood up without him even seeming to notice that I was still in the room. I walked over and placed my hand on his back to comfort him. His six foot five inch frame yielded to my touch. He towered over me as he slowly turned to face me. As I looked up at him, his beautiful brown eyes seemed to look through me.

It was just as I had thought; talking about his wife had brought him to tears. I suppose I should have been worried that he still loved her so much, but instead it made me want to know more about this man who was a giant amongst men during the day and a gentle giant by night. I wanted to know what that kind of love was like.

As he placed his arms around my shoulders I began to slowly sway to the music that seemed to be the perfect backdrop to the quietness of the kitchen. It felt comfortable in his arms, but was he holding me or Celine?

When the music stopped we continued to dance. I smiled as I looked up at him. He looked down at me and gave me a beautiful, sexy, closed lip grin. *He's dancing with me.* In one smooth movement he took me by the hand and led me to his family room. I cringed at the thought of what might be on his mind...making love? The energy in the room was energized. I felt we had connected, and I liked it...a lot. Hayes stopped in front of the fireplace. I imagine each picture had been left on the mantle as they were placed there by his late wife.

"This is my daughter, Leah, when she was a little girl. This is Leah and her husband Solomon."

"She's beautiful, Hayes. She looks a lot like her father. Your son-in-law is very handsome too. You like him?"

"He's extremely good to her and my grandchildren. He's good to her and good for her. She's very strong willed – takes a whole lot of man to handle her."

"Where'd she get that from?"

"Her mom." Hayes laughed.

I pointed to the next picture. "And these gorgeous young men are..."

"Those are my sons, Evan and Ethan."

"Twins? No, that's right; you told me they were a year apart."

"But their mom always insisted they dress alike. I guess she had a master plan because those boys grew to be as close as twins. That picture was taken when they were about eight or nine years old. They wanted to be out of control, but Celine wouldn't stand for it." He chuckled.

"So, how old are the boys in this picture?" I pointed to an ornate brown frame.

"I think that was right after they graduated from college. Ethan took extra classes, so that he and his brother could graduate at the same time. Their mom had just told them they could now get their own place and stop coming home interrupting our solitude. They were laughing at her when she took that picture."

My mouth fell open as I looked at the next picture. I took it off the mantle to thoroughly examine it. "This must be Celine. Hayes, she is absolutely breathtaking."

"Thank you…inside she was twice as beautiful and she had a heart as big as the world."

I looked at the picture of the woman and experienced a brief moment of superficial insecurity. *I pale in comparison to her.*

Hayes must have been reading my thoughts.

"I would never compare the two of you. It wouldn't be fair, for so many reasons. I was privileged to share 28 years with her. Well, actually 32 years because we dated all through college, but, let me tell you, the first time I saw you I felt exactly the same way I felt the first time I saw Celine."

I looked at him and blushed as he continued. "The

first time I saw you I thought, 'Who is she?' I had to find out who you were. One of the secretaries told me your name. She also told me you were just as intelligent and nice as you were beautiful...and that you were young. She kind of slipped that in there to let me know, in her opinion I'm sure, that I was too old to pursue you. My nose has been wide open ever since. I wanted to follow you around like a schoolboy. As I'm sure you noticed, I walked by your office quite frequently...even when I didn't have to. Just to get a glimpse of you made my day. It still does. I found out that you were very well spoken of, and extremely sought after around the office. I think I saw you outside with a young man once. I was hoping it was your brother, until you kissed him. I sat back and waited, hoping I would get a chance to talk with you alone...one day."

"So, that's why you almost got your hand crushed in the elevator door."

"I would have broken my leg if I had known it would mean that you'd be here right now."

"You know, you could have come in my office and talked to me..."

"About what? I didn't want to make a fool of myself. Rejection can be very painful, not to mention humiliating."

I hadn't noticed Hayes moving closer to me until I found myself almost looking straight up at him.

He looked down at me and smiled a boyish grin. "Thank you."

"For what?"

He gently cupped my hands inside of his massive hands and kissed them for each thing he was thankful for. "For running late that day...for dinner that evening...for entertaining my rusty advances toward you the last week or so...for being here right now...for allowing me to talk about my wife. I haven't talked about her with anyone other than my children and a psychologist in the last four years. I couldn't. So, thank you."

I began to speak, but, still cupping both of my hands he placed his finger on my lips.

"I feel like I can let her go now. Vada, you make me feel like...anything is possible. Like I can do this and it's really okay."

"Hayes...I mean...what do I say? To say you're welcome sounds so mundane and insignificant." I continued to think how beautifully odd it was that I had, just the night before, said almost the exact words to Dee, that Hayes made me feel like anything was possible.

"Trust me, it wouldn't be insignificant. I know I just laid a lot on you. I hope I'm not scaring you away. That's just how I feel. I've grown to realize that you have to seize the opportunity to say what you feel, when you feel it. If you don't, you might not ever get the chance to do it."

I took my hands from his grasp, looked up at him and motioned for him to bend down closer. When he did, I placed my hands on either side of his sun-kissed face and whispered in his ear. "You're welcome."

Then I gently kissed him.

Chapter 9

May 14, 2012

Last week was great! Spent lots of time with Hayes. Talked and talked and talked. Kissed him for the first time. I'll never forget the look on his face afterwards. He was trying to look cool, but I could tell he wanted to do it again. Dee tripped when I told her. She was more excited about the kiss than I was. Well, not really...

Hayes Vishmell Hayes Vishmell Hayes Vishmell – Vada Vishmell...Vada Jade Vishmell...VJ Vishmell...sounds kind of Jewish. ☺

I don't know what else to say about him. Okay, so it's not a superficial attraction for someone who I occasionally see. I'm really attracted to this man. My father used to love my mother like Hayes loved his wife. At least, that's what I used to think. I suppose I'll be meeting Hayes' children soon. I'm 33 years old and I want this to be my opportunity to really know what it's like to be in love and to have the kind of man I thought my dad was. I'm tripping, but I'll be all right. Maybe I'll call Hayes from the car on my way to work. It would be nice to hear his voice this morning.

THANKFUL FOR: possibilities...

———

I couldn't find my secretary after I arrived at work, so I had to make the copies for my 11 o'clock meeting myself. Not a problem. I knew how to work the copier, but I sure could have used the time to review the case file again. As I stood over the copier, considering what to do next, I heard a familiar voice.

"Do you know how to operate that machine, Ms. Bassett?"

I was prepared to shoot back a really sarcastic comment until I realized who it was.

"Oh, good morning, Mr. Vishmell. Of course I know how to work a copier. Why wouldn't I?"

The door to the copy room closed behind him as he laughed.

He sauntered towards me with those sexy bowlegs I'm so fond of. "Of course you do, but I very seldom see you away from your desk. You're either pushing papers or on the phone with a client."

I felt my body temperature rising as though I was blushing. "Mr. Vishmell, I assure you, I am extremely versatile and quite capable of handling a copier." I offered him a friendly smile.

"I'm sure you are." He bit on his bottom lip as he looked at me and continued to walk in my direction.

I blushed even more as I noticed two people passing the large picture window of the copy room. Both of them did double-takes as they glanced in the room and saw me and Hayes talking.

"I really don't recall ever seeing you in here before either, Counselor."

With his back to the door, instead of responding immediately, his eyes searched my face. "I want to kiss you."

As I momentarily turned my attention away from him and glanced at the window, the papers I was clinching fell from my hands. Hayes quickly reacted and caught them before they hit the floor, leaving very little space between the two of us.

"I want you to kiss me." My words came out as little more than a whisper.

"First chance I get today I will."

"…and I'll let you."

We stood there holding the papers at either end.

I felt it necessary to interrupt our dialogue. "I think I better go ahead and put these papers on the copier. We're about to draw a crowd. I've seen a couple of people walk by several times. I'm sure they're waiting to see what we're going to do next. You know, folks are going to start talking."

He chuckled. "They already are." He abruptly changed the subject. "Not assuming that you were going to have lunch with me, but I can't do lunch today. Can we meet for dinner?"

"Of course…"

"I want to introduce you to my children. The boys will be in town tonight and Leah and Solomon said they were available too. I'm sorry that it's such short notice, but I would really like for them to meet you."

"We're moving rather quickly aren't we?"

"Have to…time doesn't stand still for anyone."

Hayes raised his eyebrows and smiled.

"Call me and tell me where and when and I'll be there. In the meantime, these papers aren't going to get copied if I just keep standing here…and I do have an 11 o'clock meeting."

Before he turned to walk away he gave me a mischievous grin. "I still want that kiss."

I lowered my head and looked up at him. "…and I still want you to have it."

As he opened the door to leave he looked back and laughed. "Ms. Bassett, if you would do that before the end of the day I'd greatly appreciate it."

"I'll make it my business to take care of that before I leave work today, Mr. Vishmell." I made sure I said it loud enough for the people standing outside the room to hear.

He continued to smile as he walked away. The small crowd of others who had been attempting to discreetly watch us quietly dispersed and scampered away like cockroaches.

———

Before lunch, Hayes called and left a message asking me to meet him at his house at 6 o'clock. After lunch Dee kept calling and amusingly referring to me as the step-mom. Not funny, not really. I should never have told her about meeting his kids. The strange thing about the whole situation is that because of their ages, I probably should have been hanging out with them instead of with him. So I'm now on my way to meet them. Who would have thought I'd one day be meeting the adult children of someone I'm dating? I was nervous, but excited. I wondered if he had ever introduced his kids to any of the other women he had gone out with. I knew he had dated, but I didn't really know how much. Maybe I'd find a way to tactfully ask him about it. I got the impression he was very discriminating, but, then again, he is a man. After his wife's death I'm sure women came out of the woodwork to comfort him. Women can be so lecherous and conniving. They'll attack when they smell the scent of a man like Hayes: successful, intelligent, financially secure, and handsome.

In his voicemail message, he had asked me to park my car in his garage and enter the house through the garage. So, I did as I was asked to do. It looked like nobody else had arrived yet. *Maybe they're running late.* I looked at my watch and realized I was early. I got out of my car and rang the doorbell before entering the house.

"Hayes." I didn't want to walk in on him and surprise him, so I slowly made my way through the room.

I could hear him coming towards the kitchen.

"Is that you, VJ?"

"Yes, Counselor…"

He walked up to me and hugged me like we hadn't seen each other all day. He held onto me like I imagined I should be held. I couldn't see them, but I knew his eyes were closed.

"I really enjoyed work today. I felt like a young buck when I finally snuck that kiss from you this afternoon."

I tilted my head back and looked up at his face. "I enjoyed that myself. It was nice...very nice."

"I could get use to that, if you allowed me to." His eyes smiled as he spoke.

I bit the inside of my lip and continued to look up at him as he looked down at me. I found myself almost hypnotized by the movement of his beautiful, full lips as his eyes searched every inch of my face. I closed my eyes and nestled my forehead into his chest. I soon felt Hayes' hand lifting my chin, so I opened my eyes to look at him.

I again studied his lips as he spoke.

"Maybe I'm just an old cat taken by a young woman, but I could see myself being in love with you one day soon, Miss Bassett."

I didn't wait for him to kiss me. I put my arms around his neck and pulled him down to meet my lips.

"I assure you, I can handle that."

When our lips parted we stood and looked at each other. I wondered what he was thinking because his eyes seemed glazed over. His kisses were something new, something I had never experienced with William. William was a good kisser, but not like Hayes. Not at all like Hayes.

We both came to our senses when we heard a key in the door.

"That must be the kids." He spoke in a baritone whisper, but he didn't release me.

I smiled. "Maybe you should let me go. I really don't think it would make a good first impression if they found us in the kitchen all hugged up."

"You might be right," he laughed.

Gently grabbing both of my shoulders he kissed me on the forehead. "I don't know what to do with my hands now that I'm not holding you."

After excusing myself to go to the bathroom to freshen up my lipstick, I glanced back at him over my shoulder. "You can hold onto me later."

Hayes laughed that laugh again. "Well, if that's the case, I'm going to ask the kids to leave as soon as they finish eating dinner, like at 6:30. So, hurry up in the bathroom."

I giggled like a school girl. "Hayes."

I could hear his daughter calling him, so I hurried to the bathroom.

———

Dinner was very nice and Hayes' grandchildren were extremely well behaved. Owen, the baby, ate a couple of bites and went straight to sleep. Lydia was so taken by her Poppu, as she refers to him, not much else going on at the table mattered to her. That's exactly how I felt, not much else going on mattered, except Hayes. Every now and then I would steal a glance at him and he would already be sitting there looking at me, smiling a different kind of smile, and I understood exactly what it meant. It was warm and comfortable at the table with him and his family. At least twice, that I noticed, his daughter caught us. And each time, I thought I heard her take a deep sigh. Maybe it was my imagination, maybe not. If I were in her shoes I might have been more than a little annoyed by my dad bringing some young 'thang' to dinner, but, then again, I don't consider myself some young 'thang.' Leah didn't know that yet though. As the night went on, it appeared as if she was getting more and more aggravated. And why shouldn't she be? I was sort of like the other woman.

Evan's and Ethan's travels and newest pursuits dominated the dinner conversation. At one point during dinner, though, I could have sworn they were checking me out. In spite of that, dinner went as well as to be expected. Everyone was on his or her best behavior. After dinner Hayes' sons retired to the family room. Hayes attempted to clear the table, but both Leah and I insisted he join the guys in the other room. Lydia was more than glad to finally have her poppu's full attention. Hayes walked up to me as if he was going to kiss me, but caught himself and stopped – Lydia was trying to pull him into the other room anyway. Leah, while clearing the table, seemed to still have her eye on me…and he knew it.

In the kitchen, I attempted to make conversation with Leah about how well her dad cooked. She was more than pleasant, but obviously distant.

"Leah, is there something you want to say? You seem just a little, I don't know, uncomfortable with me?"

She glared at me, almost challenging me. "Is it that obvious?"

I wanted to rid her of any concerns she might have. So, I nervously broached the subject that was so heavily hanging over our heads. "Yeah, and I can understand why. I'm sure you're trying to figure out what I'm doing with your father?"

"Hmph! That's an understatement, but you're right. Look, you seem nice enough – young for my dad – but nice enough. I really do want to talk more about this, but I just don't think this is the venue for it. You're probably thinking it's none of my business anyway, because my dad is, well, my dad, and he can do what he wants to do. You're partially right. He is my dad, but he's been through a lot the last few years and I'm not going to let anybody hurt him, if I can help it. Do you think we can meet for lunch sometime this week and really talk?"

As much as I hated to admit it, Leah was right. I wanted to be pissed off because Hayes is more than grown; he's 52 years old with grown children and little grandchildren – and who did she think she was questioning our relationship? I chuckled because I saw a little of myself in her. I knew I would be just as protective of my daddy given the same situation. Now that I thought about it, I was in a pretty similar situation. It was just a matter of time before I met her, my dad's 'baby mama,' and I knew she had to be much younger than my dad.

I stopped what I was doing and looked at Leah. "Sure, lunch sounds good. You know, I understand how you feel. I want you and your brothers to get to know me; so that you can be assured that I'm not some gold digger. I like him a lot, Leah, and I think I know him well enough to say he would be glad that you and I are talking. Of course, I'm not going to run and tell him that we're meeting for lunch, but I know that it's important to him that we all get to know each other."

Her eyes softened. She had let her defenses down, just a bit. There was absolutely no reason to trust me because she knew her dad was a good catch and we both knew that in older man younger woman relationships the hook was usually the sex. What she didn't know was that I was a virgin.

———

Hayes didn't have to usher everybody out of the house like I thought he was going to do. Around 8:45'ish Evan announced that he and his brother had to leave because they had other plans. Solomon thought he and Leah should leave to get the kids into bed. That was going to leave me and Hayes just the way he wanted it...alone. Before Leah left she and I traded phone numbers, so that we could make arrangements to meet for lunch some time during the week. I was included in the family's round of hugs and exchange of pleasantries. As soon as everybody was out of the house, Hayes pent me up against the kitchen door and kissed me like a sex starved schoolboy. I wondered if I brought this out of him or if this was just the tip of the iceberg.

"Whoa, cowboy; let a girl catch her breath. Where'd that come from?"

"I wanted to kiss you all through dinner, but I didn't know how we could discreetly leave the table without drawing attention to ourselves. I love...I loved the way you got along with my children. Good sign. Good sign. I'm going to have to talk with my boys, though. They were checking you out."

"Why do you say that?"

"I know my boys."

I laughed. "I'm flattered; old enough to get the dad and young enough to date the sons, too. I would say that ain't half bad, huh?"

Hayes laughed and gave me a one arm hug as we walked over to his wine cooler to get a bottle of wine.

Chapter 10

May 22, 2012

Leah and I are going to have lunch today. "Hooray!" I guess...I'm sure it's going to be fine. I hope she doesn't attempt to run me off or try to talk me out of being with her dad. I ain't scared of her. ☺ I'm so thankful to have met a man like Hayes. I think we can fall in love, get married, have a baby or two then start our own law firm, "Vishmell and Vishmell." In the meantime, I have to pass the daughter test. Leah's cool, but a little over protective, I think. I wonder if I come off like that with my dad. I hope not.

Speaking of my daddy, I really miss him. I haven't seen him or talked with him since lunch with him and Monyet. Hayes told me I needed to work that out...soon. From what my mom has told me, I understand my dad doesn't live too far away. It's just that I haven't taken the time to find out where. Guess I'm still coming to grips with the divorce. He called me over the weekend. Said he missed me and would love to see me. He gave me his new phone number and asked me to call him sometime. I told him I would. I also told him I was sure we'd see each other soon. I don't think I'm ready to call him at home and talk with the other woman yet, though. I might be a lot younger than Hayes, but at least I'm not breaking up a happy family to be with him.

THANKFUL FOR: Hayes…for talking with my dad, and for getting this conversation with Leah out of the way

———

It feels like I'm getting caught at every single red light there is on the road. I didn't want to be late for lunch. I have to admit, I'm a little anxious. I know I want Hayes…and Hayes wants me. I'm sure Leah will see that I'm not trying to take advantage of her dad.

I parked my car and nervously walked into the restaurant. I contemplatively approached the hostess to get a table or to find out if Leah was already there; Leah stood and waved me over before I had an opportunity to get a word out.

I smiled at the hostess. "Thanks, I see my party."

I didn't know whether to hug Leah or shake her hand, so as I sat down I merely began talking. "Good to see you again. I hope I didn't have you waiting long."

She smiled a very sincere, toothy smile. "No, I haven't been here long. The sitter got to my house early, so I hurried and left while she distracted Lydia. I said all of that to say, you weren't late, I was a little early."

Fortunately, our waitress arrived with our menus and took our drink orders. I had already run out of things to say, but it was apparent Leah was ready to talk.

"So, how long have you been seeing my dad?"

"I thought we would at least order first before we jumped into it." I chuckled.

"I don't mean to come on so strong. It's just that, I love my father. He's been through a lot the last four

90

years and I really don't think I could take him being hurt again. And if I can help it, I'm not going to let that happen."

Again, the waitress interrupted to serve our drinks and to take our lunch orders. We both gave her unassuming smiles, hoping she would be motivated to leave our table a little quicker, so that we could get back to the matter at hand.

"Well, Leah, like I told you the other night, I'm very fond of your father. Actually, I'm more than fond of him; I'm extremely attracted to him and obviously the feeling is mutual. And to answer your question, we've only been seeing each other for almost a month. So, really, at this point anything can still happen."

Our conversation was briefly interrupted again as the waitress served our food. We both thanked her. As I took my first mouthful of food I realized that, though Leah may think I'm 'nice enough,' she still might not want me seeing her dad. My thought was cut short as she began to speak.

"I mean, really, woman-to-woman, what can my dad do for you? You're what, 35 years old? My dad's 52; don't you think he's a bit old for you?"

I slowly chewed my food and thoughtfully considered what I would say before looking up at her and attempting to reply as calmly as possible.

"First of all, I'm only 33, just a couple of years older than you. And I'm sure you don't really want to discuss this woman-to-woman because the real question would be 'what can I do for him?' Like you said, he's considerably older than I am, so that makes me the little young 'thang' – supposedly, fun loving, lively, entertaining, endless amounts of energy…particularly, in comparison to a 52 year old man, right? I know what I have to offer your father and I can even see how he fits into my life. I'd like to believe that I know what he has to offer me—as a man. Perhaps you should be asking your father what he wants with a 33-year-old woman. Don't you think that's a more viable question? I can assure you that I don't want his money—I have my own; I don't want his house—I have one of those too, not too much smaller than his, I might add; and I don't want his nice little black Jaguar—you may not have noticed, but I drive a very nice baby blue BMW.

Sensing she had struck a nerve, Leah angrily replied, "I'm not trying to piss you off. I'm just very adamant about my father's happiness."

"Don't you think you're overstepping your boundaries, just a little bit? He is a grown man. Do your brothers feel the same way about me as you do?"

Leah took her right hand and swatted at the air, as if to shoo away a fly. "Of course not, why would they be mad that their old man has a young sex kitten to help him deal with whatever stress or residual sadness he might be dealing with?"

She obviously felt vindicated by that jab. It was clear, from the smirk on her face, that she was making a blatant attack of my character. She smugly began eating her meal again. So, it was out. Leah did think the relationship between Hayes and I was purely sexual and that I was gold digging, money grubbing freak. My feelings were hurt, but as an attorney I was taught to never let them see you sweat. Though, I had to really tell myself to play it cool, calm, and collected because this wasn't work. This was personal. I also had to remind myself that this was Hayes' daughter that I was talking with, and, more importantly, I needed to play friendly with her because, in spite of how she felt or what she thought, I was going to be with him. Even though, what I really wanted to do was throw her glass of lemonade in her face.

I put my fork down and stared at her until she looked back up at me. "Look, I can assure you, my relationship with your father is not about sex. We've never been intimate in that way…in any way sexually. As a matter of fact, I'm a virgin. Not that any of this is your business."

I thought she was going to choke. I had to jump up and run around the table to help her, but Leah grabbed her drink with one hand and waved me back to my seat with the other.

I was compelled to ask, "Are you all right?"

She coughed a little to clear her throat and with a strained voice asked, "What do you mean you're a virgin?"

"I mean I've never had sex before."

In utter disbelief, she continued to query me. "How is that even possible? You expect me to believe that you're 33 years old and you've 'NEVER' had sex?"

"Leah, I'm not concerned with whether or not you

believe me; it's the truth. I'm a daddy's girl just like you. My dad and my mother taught me the value of waiting, saving myself. They taught me that abstinence is a lifestyle. As a matter of fact, my dad assured me that if I could master that I could be successful in anything else that I might choose to do in life. He also taught me that because 'I' am the prize, not every man that I met or dated in my life would deserve the prize. I truly believe that, with all my heart and soul. I probably have some overly romantic notions about sex…making love, whatever, but that's okay because the only person that I'll share those notions with is my husband."

Leah apparently was not expecting this turn in the conversation.

So I continued. "You know, even though I sort of understand where you're coming from, I still feel very strongly that you're overstepping all of the proverbial boundaries, because there's a difference between getting to know the woman your dad is involved with and attempting to control who that woman might be. I don't think Hayes – your dad – would appreciate the latter."

Leah sat back in her chair and contemplatively gazed at me before hesitantly nodding her head. "You're right, he wouldn't, but my interest in my dad's relationship isn't unwarranted. It's been a while ago, but I walked in on him and his date one night. She was going for it. I felt sorry for her. Here she was trying to seduce the man and he was acting like he was completely turned off. It was crazy watching her with my dad. He finally had to embarrass her and tell her that she had too much to drink. He offered to take her home after insisting she have some coffee. She was crying and asking him why he didn't want her. It was wild."

"I can't believe you stayed and watched. How did he explain that whole episode?" I was curious for more than the obvious reasons.

"He didn't. Believe it or not, it was so quick that I left the house and never even mentioned it to him."

In an act of solidarity, I jokingly mocked her. "Oh, so you and I have a secret, huh?"

She smiled. "I guess we do."

It was the sincerest smile I had received from her since we met.

In our chorus of laughter, we had seemingly established a newfound friendship. I assured her that I didn't want to hurt her dad any more than I wanted to be hurt by him. We ended lunch with promises that she would have me over soon, and I would have her and her family over, as well.

———

May 25, 2012

End of another wonderful week!

Recap: Lunch with Leah on Wednesday. Started out shaky, ended with nothing but love. Dee thought I should have put Leah in her place a little stronger than I did. She said I should have grabbed her by her shoulders and said, "Do you realize you're talking to your future step-mother," and then I should have smacked some sense into her. Dee is crazy! She said she wasn't surprised that Leah came on so strong or that she thought my relationship with her dad was about sex. Dee wanted to know what else I could be but a boy-toy for a 52 year old man. She also said if it had been her sitting at that table, Leah would have gotten up and run away by the time she finished telling her the truth, "woman-to-woman." She would have told her, "Yeah, it is about sex…sex in the kitchen…in the bedroom….in the car…during lunch…at night…every day." She said better me than her because Leah would have gone home and sat in a corner rocking and sucking her thumb. Dee obviously has some issues she needs to work out.

Leah and I agreed that we wouldn't mention lunch to her dad. She was embarrassed and very apologetic as we left the restaurant. I'm glad Hayes had mentioned how strong her personality was. It could have been enough to turn me off if I hadn't been forewarned. Anyway, he and I are doing fine. I never get tired of talking to him or seeing him. Guess that's the best part of new relationships. I hope that never changes. I like it.

Having dinner with my mom tonight; I think it's time I told her about Hayes. I've struggled with that because he's only a few years younger than her. He probably should be dating her instead of me. Here I am with him and she has nobody. I can't stand my dad for that. Everything always leads back to him. Always!

Got to get out of here and go to work…

THANKFUL FOR: new beginnings, meeting Hayes'
children, lunch with his daughter, dinner with my mom
& for Hayes…

———

"VJ, I have a Mrs. Butler on the line. She says she would like to briefly speak with you regarding community property."

"Carolyn, do you know if it's Adelle Butler?"

"Yes, it is, as a matter of fact."

"Okay, put her through. Thanks!"

"Mrs. Butler, it's always good to hear from you. It's been a while. How's Mr. Butler?"

"That's what I'm calling about, Ms. Bassett. He died about a month ago and I'm not sure what I need to do about the house and the cars that are in both of our names."

"I'm very sorry to hear that your husband passed away. Did he have a will?"

"No, that's the problem. I know that there are laws, but does that mean I have to go down to the courthouse and put the property and the cars in my name? I've talked with a few people in the clerk's office, but they don't seem to know the answers to any of my questions. So, I thought I better call you. I don't know what to do."

"I'm glad you called. Property held as community property doesn't automatically pass to the surviving spouse unless there is a written agreement of survivorship regarding the property; which it sounds like you don't have. I remember you and your husband mentioning children to me in the past. Whether you inherit your husband's share of the community property will depend on whether or not he has any children that are not also yours. If he does, then all of his children will inherit his share of his community property, but if all of his children are also your children then you inherit his share. You may want to make an appointment to come in so that we can discuss that, as well as determine if the estate qualifies for small estate treatment. If it doesn't, you'll need to have a formal administration and determination of heirship to transfer title of the properties you mentioned."

"I knew I should have called you sooner, but it's taking me a while to get myself together. Hilliard did have two kids before we married. I don't suppose they care about the house and the cars since I'm still living, but I don't know. They haven't made a fuss yet. How soon can I come in to see you?"

"Carolyn keeps my calendar, so I'm going to have to transfer you back to her. I'll ask her to get you in here as quickly as my calendar will allow. And again, Mrs. Butler, I am so sorry to hear about Mr. Butler. I look forward to seeing you soon. We're going to get things all straightened out for you."

"Thank you so much, Ms. Bassett. You're such a sweet girl. I look forward to seeing you soon."

"Okay, hold on. I'm going to transfer you now. Take care."

As I transferred Mrs. Butler back to Carolyn, it occurred to me that these were the kind of issues that could come up if my dad dies. I thought again about how many lives he had complicated without even giving it any consideration.

Carolyn's voice brought me back to reality. "VJ?"

"I'm sorry. Would you, please, schedule an appointment for Mrs. Butler to come in as soon as possible to discuss Community Property, Estate Treatment, etc? You'll probably need to block out about two hours. Also, please confirm her address and send her flowers with a card expressing my regrets, in behalf of the firm, for the loss of her husband. Thanks, okay?"

"Yes, ma'am, I'll take care of it."

A voice came out of nowhere. "That was very thoughtful, Ms. Bassett."

I didn't realize Hayes had been standing in my doorway watching me.

I smiled a sassy smile. "How long have you been standing there spying on me?"

"Not long. Just long enough to hear you arrange an appointment and flowers for a client. That was a nice touch. Do you do that often? And since when did my observing you become spying?"

"Of course, I always do that when the occasion arises. Your secretary probably takes care of that for you. Do you have time to come in, so we can talk? Please, close the door behind you."

As he closed the door I got up out of my chair from behind my desk and walked over to him.

"What's going on here, Ms. Bassett? It appears that this is about to become a possible sexual harassment situation."

"Uh, huh…you're correct. What are you going to do about it?"

Hayes slowly walked towards me and stopped when there was no more space between us. He looked down at me as he wrapped his arms around my waist. I closed my eyes and inhaled in his cologne, which was uniquely Hayes Vishmell.

"Put your arms around my neck." He commanded.

I looked at him. "Like this?"

"Uh, huh. Now, close your eyes again."

"Why?"

"I want to show you how to harass me properly."

I closed my eyes as he instructed. I felt his soft, warm, full lips, parting my lips with his tongue. When we finished I opened my eyes to find him looking at me.

I could have stood there longer, but I didn't want to create a riotous situation in the hallway.

"You know, we can't stay hold up in here for the rest of the day. Not that I would mind, but eventually curiosity would get the best of the folks that I know are gathering outside of my door."

"I don't care. I'm in here with VJ Bassett. I've waited too long to be with you to care." Then he softly kissed my forehead, the tip of my nose, and then my lips. "VJ, I'm not one for long mergers. We need to close this deal, you know?"

I was perplexed. "What are you saying?"

"I know it's only been a month, but I want you in my life and I don't think that's going to change in the foreseeable future. I don't want to run you away, but I guess I'm asking you to marry me without asking you to marry me. At least, consider that that's what I want for us, okay?"

I was still confused, but I managed to respond anyway. "That's fair enough. I can do that – consider. Oh, and I'm not going anywhere, Mr. Vishmell."

"I suppose I would need to meet your family first, huh?" Then he laughed that beautiful baritone laugh …from his gut.

"Yeah, I don't think it would go over to well if I introduced you to my parents at the wedding. That wouldn't be appropriate at all."

He smiled. "You're right. Well, let's do what we need to do, so that I can meet your folks. I'm available tonight."

"Wow. I am having dinner with my mom tonight. So, I'll tell you what I'll do. I'll make arrangements with her tonight for you to meet her this weekend. How 'bout that?"

"…and your father?"

"Give me a little time to work on that, okay?" My reply was tentative at best.

"I'm not going to give you long."

"I know…"

Just as we were about to kiss again, my intercom buzzed. "VJ?"

"Yes, Carolyn."

"I have a call for you…"

I tried not to sound annoyed as I rolled my eyes and

sighed. "Would you, please, take a message? Tell whoever it is that I'll call them back in about ten or fifteen minutes?"

"Okay…"

"Thanks, Carolyn."

I focused my attention back on Hayes. "Mr. Vishmell, I think I better end our social hour and return that call."

"You work too hard. All work and no play, makes….."

"Whatever. I'll call you from my car after I leave the office."

We shared another long, lingering kiss before Hayes turned to leave my office. As he reached for the door I stopped him.

"Wait. Let me wipe the lipstick off your lips."

I took my finger and gently rubbed his lips. When I finished he opened the door and looked back and smiled.

"As usual, great work, Ms. Bassett." The small crowd of others that had been lurking outside my door all but stumbled over each other as they attempted to quickly disband.

———

"Mom, you outdid yourself tonight."

After putting away the leftovers and loading the dishwasher, we walked arm in arm to the family room.

"Then why'd you stop coming over, silly girl?" My mom wrinkled her face disapprovingly.

I acted baffled and pretended to think. "Oh, yeah…I

don't know."

We both laughed.

"Actually, Mom, I do know why I haven't been coming over much."

"Don't tell me, let me guess. You and William made up?"

"No, that's not going to happen, but I am seeing someone."

"Stop being so cat and mouse with me. Tell me about him."

"Okay, he works at the firm."

"Oh, Vada, those office romances never work. Do you think maybe you're on the rebound? You have so much going on right now...your dad...breaking up with William. Did Dee set y'all up?"

"No, Mother, it's not like that. And anyway, Dee is my friend. She wouldn't just throw me to the wolves like that. This guy is someone that I've been checking out for some time...and he's been checking me out too, but the opportunity for us to go out just never presented itself until now. Anyway, like I was saying, he's about six foot five, 230 or so pounds, chocolate brown, brown eyes, close cut, black hair..."

My mom clapped her hands. "You had me at six foot five, sweetie."

We both laughed.

"Mom, you're so silly. And...he's 52 years old."

Looking distressed, my mother interrupted. "Oh, Vada, do you have some kind of father complex now? He's what, 19 years older than you are?

Vada…Vada…Vada…"

"What? No, it's just ironic that we got together now. If William and I hadn't broken up I never would have gone out with Hayes. He's good for me, though, Mom. I think, no, I know you'll like him. It's important to me that you like him."

"Wait a minute. He's 52. Is he married?

"Give me some credit. Geesh, lady, my mother and father raised me better than that. You know?"

"Well, why would a 52 year old man be single? He ain't one of them 'DL' brothers is he? And you do know he is the rebound man, right?"

"You need to stop watching all those lady talk shows."

We both doubled over with laughter, even though we knew the possibilities of meeting one of those bogus brothers seemed more real than ever these days.

"Mom, he's a widower. His wife died from cancer four years ago. They had been together for 32 years…and I don't think he's my rebound man. Things just happen like they happen sometimes."

"I'm not even going to say anything about the fact that they were together almost as long as you've been on this earth."

"Okay, don't. Anyway, he has three children: a daughter, 31 years old, and two sons, 28 and 29 years old."

"So, that means, not only will you be the step-mom, but you'll make a great playmate for his children."

"Oh, you are so full of jokes tonight. His children are

great and he's wonderful. I had lunch with his daughter a few days ago."

My mom fought the urge to sound like a psychologist, even though she ended up sounding just like one anyway. "I bet that was interesting."

"That's an understatement. Initially, I thought she wanted to attack me, but by the end of lunch we were buddies."

"I bet she was really protective of that ole' father of hers, huh?"

"She really was. She all but accused me of taking advantage of him – like he couldn't be taking advantage of me. I thought about throwing her lemonade in her face after she practically accused me of being a whore. She didn't say the word, but that's what she was implying."

"This man must be something special. His daughter is all in his business trying to protect him – attacking your character to make sure that he doesn't get hurt." Her words tinged with a bit of sarcasm.

"She sounds a little over protective, if you ask…" My voice trailed off. "Mother, are you trying to make a point? If you are…I'm not like that about Daddy."

"Uh, huh, I know…"

"I'm not. So, anyway, when would you like to meet him?"

"Tomorrow would be fine. Vada, if it doesn't work out between y'all I might need to check him out for myself. Maybe his daughter won't have a problem with me."

"Mother, that's not funny. You…are…sick."

Chapter 11

May 26, 2012

Hayes and I are officially a couple. We have planned a trip to Barbados. I think it was something Hayes had been thinking about for a minute or two. He sprang it on me during dinner with my mother. We're leaving tomorrow. He said it shouldn't be a problem for me to call in and get someone else to handle my clients. Did I neglect to mention my mom and her best friend, Cecilia, are going to go also? As ridiculous as that sounds to Dee, that's how we're going to do it. I will have my own room, Hayes will have his own room, and my mom and her Cecilia will share a room. We're going there for six days and five nights. Of course, Hayes and I don't plan on spending every waking moment with my mom and Cecilia. They'll be off doing their thing and we'll be off doing ours, but we will meet for dinner or lunch. At least, that's the plan.

My mom loves Hayes. Thinks he's the best thing since chocolate milk. Wanted to know why she couldn't have met him first. I told her it was because he was younger than her. She agreed, but added, "Not by much…"

Hayes adores Lois Bassett. After dinner he told me that he could have dated my mother if he met her first. They're both sick…and if I must be honest about it, I don't find it the least bit funny! They seem to have become fast friends. How weird is it that my boyfriend is practically my mother's age? Shoot, they come from the same era. They probably have more in common than he and I do. How crazy is that?

I still haven't introduced him to my dad. As a matter of fact, I haven't even told my dad that William and I broke up. My mom hasn't told him anything either. She says it's my business and I can tell him myself when I get ready.

Dee is planning my wedding. I've only known Hayes for a month...and she's planning our wedding. Funny thing is I think he really might be the one. It doesn't hurt that he's pre-proposed already. That's what really got Dee going. He and I are going to make beautiful babies – so she says. It's still early in the game, but I know something good when I see it.

THANKFUL FOR: Mom liking Hayes, Hayes liking Mom, and Dee's great sense of humor

————

On May 27, 2012, we arrived in Montego Bay, Jamaica at 8:40 a.m. for our two-hour layover. The airport was far from what I had expected. My mom and Miss Cecilia were like giddy tourists. Hayes walked with his hand in the small of my back as he led us into one of the airport restaurants. He thought we all needed drinks, nice cold rum punch...at 9 o'clock in the morning.

After just a few sips my mom was laughing like a

schoolgirl. It appeared that, amongst other things, Hayes' forte was also entertaining women. I shouldn't have been so surprised that Mom and Ms. Cecilia were so enthralled by him. Ms. Cecilia couldn't keep her eyes off of him. I knew she was harmless, but I thought I might have to have a little talk with her before our trip was over. It was either that or keep her away from him whenever she's drinking.

Hayes affectionately squeezed the back of my neck. "What are you thinking about, sweetie?"

I looked at him and smiled, "Nothing, really, just absorbing the scenery."

He put his arm around me and I closed my eyes as he kissed me on my left temple.

———

Barbados was beautiful. Our Air Jamaica flight landed at Grantley Adams International Airport in Bridgetown, Barbados at 3:50 p.m. As we exited the plane, I immediately noticed how much bluer the sky seemed than in the States and how vibrant the colors of the flowers and trees were. At first glance, I could have sworn the air was a little clearer and a little more beautiful too. The energy as we exited the plane convinced me that the trip was a great idea. Admittedly, it was a little strange to be taking a trip with someone that I hadn't known very long and even stranger to have my mother and her friend on the trip with us, but the truth is it was more than a great idea; it was an absolutely wonderful idea. I made a mental note to call

Dee later and tell her that we had to make plans to come back with her son and dad.

Hayes led us through Customs and then out to the rental car office to rent a Land Rover. I learned from him that Barbados was one of his hangouts, so he was quite comfortable driving, but he forewarned us that we might have to get adjusted to the driving habits of the locals. We immediately realized what he meant when we went around our first "roundabout." As we left the airport, Hayes also did a great job acting as our tour guide. The airport was in the parish of Christ Church, which I learned was two parishes away from where we were going to be staying. After the two hours that it took us to get our bags, go through Customs, and then get the car, we still had a bit of a ride before we would make it to our hotel.

The wind played in my short hair as I sat practically side-saddle in the front, passenger seat.

"So, Hayes, other than driving on the left side of the road, what other surprises can we look forward to while we're here?"

Mr. Vishmell looked extra sexy as he glanced over and smiled at me, the tip of his tongue playing with his front teeth. I wanted to reach over and kiss him, but, instead, I smiled back and winked my eye at him. There was definitely something to be said for the clean, fresh air in Barbados.

"Well, let's see." Hayes pondered out loud. "We've missed rush hour. It ended at about 6 o'clock. Oh, if you hear people blowing their horns they might be speaking to somebody walking or they could be saying 'excuse me, here I come.' And if somebody flashes their lights at us at an intersection or a roundabout they're probably telling us to go first."

Miss Cecilia chimed in, "Well, isn't that just too sweet? In the States any or all of that could mean get the heck out of my way. I'm coming whether you're ready or not!"

We laughed at the truthfulness of her statement. I continued to watch Hayes as he spoke, pointing out the different plants and fruit trees as we passed. We by-passed downtown Bridgetown because he said it was too congested; and we could always come back another time, though we did get a chance to see the University of the West Indies.

I gently massaged Hayes' neck and playfully quizzed him. "Since this is your world, what do you have planned for us?"

He looked at me with a raised eyebrow. "I want to take you ladies to all of my favorite restaurants for dinner; a different one each night. Lois, I thought you and Cecilia might appreciate the different flower gardens and underground caverns…"

Mom quickly butted in, "Excuse me. I know you're not trying to give us the 'old lady' tour? What's wrong with you?"

He laughed. "Lois, come on now. I think you know me better than that. VJ and I will be with you. I just thought y'all might appreciate…"

Before he could finish Miss Cecilia interrupted.

"Why?"

I palmed the back of Hayes' head. "You should stop while you're ahead. The more you talk the worse it's going to get. See, that's what happens when you let your secretary plan your vacation."

He looked over at me with a wrinkled brow. "Helen didn't plan this vacation. I did all of this myself."

Chuckling, Mom took control of the conversation. "Okay, then, after we get to the hotel and freshen up for dinner, we'll revise that itinerary."

Letting go of the stirring wheel and holding up both of his hands, Hayes conceded. "I lived in a house with a wife and a daughter, so I know when to throw in the towel. I can't win this one."

I looked over at him and chuckled. "Sure you can."

Before we knew it we had arrived at our destination...and it wasn't a hotel. It was actually a very lovely villa. As the car stopped, I admired the view. The house was situated such that there was an amazing view of the Caribbean Sea. A butler came out to the car to take our bags, while my mom and Miss Cecilia quickly went in to examine their dwelling for the next few days. Hayes walked over and placed his hand on the small of my back.

"Are you okay?"

I quickly turned and looked at him. "This is too much, Hayes..."

"What do you mean it's too much? I'm trying to win your mother over," he grinned.

"All jokes aside. I'm sure this far exceeds what my

mom and Miss Cecilia were expecting. I hadn't even…"

He put his finger on my lips. "Shhh…don't be ridiculous, VJ, this is my place."

I looked down as I pondered over the idea of spending my vacation in a place that held so many memories for him.

"What do you mean your place? Is this where you and your wife used to vacation?"

"Of course not, we came to Barbados on occasion, but we always stayed at the country club here in Sandy Lane. I bought this place after she died."

Hayes placed his hand under my chin. "Look at me. Do you think I would do that to you? I want to share some new things with you, VJ. After Celine died I bought this place to be by myself and mourn, but I quickly realized you can't mourn here. It's too beautiful. So, now, this has become all about us, you and me. No interruptions by the phone, ex-boyfriends, late wives, children – nothing that we would think about in the States. Okay?"

I bit on my bottom lip as I listened to what he was saying. "Okay."

"Now that we have that straightened out, can I get a kiss?

"Uh huh…"

———

May 27, 2012

Our first night in Barbados was phenomenal! It's hard

to believe it could even get any better. I have found this tall, dark and handsome prince, who has whisked me (my queen mother and her lady in waiting) away to his castle on an enchanted island. Speaking of which, Hayes' villa is spectacular. We really could spend the entire week right here inside the house. During dinner my mom and Miss Cecilia announced that they would be doing exactly that, staying at the villa and relaxing most of the time; and why not? There's a butler, a chef, a gardener, a maid, a laundress, and a night watchman. That's just as good as, if not better than, any four or five star hotel. In addition to having a great view of the Caribbean Sea, there's a swimming pool, five bedrooms, seven bathrooms, and any other amenity that might be necessary to have a comfortable and enjoyable getaway. Hayes said he chose the "Lady Boheme," the name of his villa, because it was beautiful, yet practical for when his children vacationed.

We had dinner at a restaurant right on the Caribbean Sea, the Bajan Blue, at the Sandy Lane Hotel. I ordered blacken flying fish with homemade sweet potatoes with tomato and water melon salsa, and tasted quite a bit of Hayes' curry chicken with coconut milk, chana steamed roti, and some other stuff. I ate so much that I had to by-pass dessert. Mom reminded Hayes that she and Miss Cecilia were still going to change his itinerary. As I mentioned before, she and Miss Cecilia loved the villa so much that they decided to spend one day with me and Hayes, and the rest of their vacation resting at the house. Hayes told them they were more than welcome to use the house anytime they wanted to in the future. He's going to make a great son-in-law. ☺

After arriving back at the villa, Hayes and I held hands and walked the beach for a while. Eventually, we stopped and sat down on the rocks. I eased my back against his chest and he wrapped his arms around me, and held me close. We didn't talk. We sat quietly and listened to the waves. Every now and then we could feel the spray from the Caribbean Sea. How flippin' romantic was that? Later, we walked upstairs to our rooms, where we both had master suites. I had a sudden head rush when we kissed and parted ways. I might lose my virginity here in Barbados. I don't think I can avoid it. Wow! How wild is that? Am I falling in love with this man or is it just the energy here?

It's about 1:30 in the morning. I wonder if Hayes is thinking about me. I might go sit out on my balcony for a little while. I feel a poem coming first, though:

> *i met a young Bajan man (who baffled me), but...now i understand why his kindness was so confusing*
>
> *it is a trait indigenous to a people where kindness is as warm as a sea-bath in the waters of the blue-green Caribbean (Sea)*
>
> *where the hue of one's skin is beauty and can be as blue-black as the tranquil night sky*

he is a son of Barbados
a land so rich it is impossible
not to take in the goodness
and your spirit be made stronger

where the quietness of time is still felt
everyday in the air of casualness and
carefreeness of its natives

home is what I feel while here,
though my feet have never once graced the
hills, roads, villages, and parishes 'afore now

i am filled with tears of joy
from having come to know a people who
touched something deep within me that feels
more like self than ever before

i've picked myself up, dusted myself off, got
at it, me again
i've passed a test of time

my heart beats stronger as the surge, the
thickness, the fire of the blood of Nigerian
ancestors has come alive in my veins
reminding me that long before i was born
i existed

sunshine so bright, colors so vibrant, music
so lively, food so good
emanating life and getting at (the business of)
living

now, then, & forever
true peace & blessings, so special

praise be to God
all praise be to Jah,
who created all things,
this spirit that fills me,
and this paradise that is she,
Barbados

THANKFUL for: Caribbean breezes, good food, and
good company

Chapter 12

The week seemed to fly by. On Tuesday, after taking the Mount Gay rum tour, visiting Orchid World, and going to Earthworks Pottery with my mom and Cecilia, Hayes and I spent the rest of the week with each other, beginning with dinner on Tuesday night. Every night the restaurants got better and better. Tuesday night we ate at The Terrace at the Cobblers Cove Hotel in St. Peter parish; Wednesday night we ate at Palm Terrace at the Royal Pavilion Hotel in St. James parish; and Thursday night we ate at Mango's By the Sea in Speightstown, St. Peter parish. My mom and Miss Cecilia did grace us with their presence by joining us for dinner on Thursday night. I found myself getting absolutely spoiled by the Caribbean food.

During the day it was no different. Wednesday morning Hayes woke me up and took me to Bridgetown for some shopping. We left there and drove to Christ Church parish to visit the Graeme Hall Nature Sanctuary. From there we drove north to the East Coast of the island to St. Joseph parish to visit Bathsheba, and then back to the house to change for dinner. Thursday was another experience. Hayes woke me up at 6:45 in the morning for a 7:30 a.m. tee time. Because he's such an avid golfer, I indulged him. I had only attempted golf a few times in my life and that was only because my dad enjoyed playing. When I was a little girl I'd go with him to the country club, but I usually stayed in the golf cart and watched. As we rode to the Sandy Lane Golf Course I looked over at Hayes and he told me it was time I learned the game.

"As a matter of fact, after we're married I'm sure there will be times when you'll want to go golfing with me. There's no point in going if you didn't know how to play."

"What if I never want to go golfing with you?"

"That would be absolutely fine. We'll need our alone time too. I won't mind if golfing is my alone time." He turned and smiled at me as he drove.

"Oh, okay, that's good – really good," I laughed.

"What's so funny about that?"

"Nothing really, I was just thinking…I could ride in the golf cart like I did with my dad, but then people might think I'm 'your daughter.'" I attempted to suppress my laughter.

"I don't see the humor in that. Imagine how people would look at us every time I walked over and put my tongue in your mouth. Not so funny now, is it?"

I hit Hayes on his arm and wrinkled up my forehead. "Why'd you say that?"

"I don't want to make light of the difference in our ages. It took me a while to pass that hurdle when I first found myself attracted to you. I never really asked you, does it bother you?"

I cocked my head to one side and seriously considered his question. "No, not in and of itself; what really bothered me, at first, was the fact that you're closer to my mother's age and now she doesn't have anybody. You really could have very well been an opportunity for her to date again. My other slight concern is how your friends might receive me, particularly your friends that were also friends with your wife – the other couples that y'all hung out with. How is that going to work? I'm sure word is getting around that you're seeing someone."

As we pulled up and stopped at valet parking, Hayes looked over at me. "I don't know. I really don't. Some of them have seen me out on dates before, but, of course, it was never anything serious. A couple of my friends have even set me up with blind dates, but I don't do well with those. Of course, none of the other women were your age, so I don't know how they're going to respond to me seeing…marrying, someone younger. I guess we'll just have to cross all of those bridges as we get to them, huh?"

I smiled back at him. "Hmph…I guess so."

"What about your friends, do you think they'll have a problem with me?

"Well, Dee, you know her, Delaney Brown-Lofton. She's absolutely on team Hayes/VJ. The rest of them, it's kind of mixed, but it's not a major topic of conversation – particularly with my female friends. Especially after Dee finished telling them how you had it going on. All they want to know is if there are any more like you at home. My guy friends, on the other hand, can't understand why I can't stay in the game for a younger man."

Before we could finish our conversation the valet

opened the door. We decided to finish the conversation later, once we were on the fairway. Because Hayes thought I might lose my cool long before the 18th tee, we only played nine holes. I wouldn't have minded playing 18 holes with him, though. If I was going to learn how to play golf, there was no better place than in Barbados. On the drive back to the villa we laughed about how many times I got birdie. Hayes thought I might turn out to be a great golfer after all.

Soon after arriving back at the house and changing clothes, we left and headed for our next adventure, snuba diving, which turned out to be a cross between snorkeling and scuba diving. I got a chance to take a lot of great under water pictures. After our snuba diving adventure it was lunch at Cocomos in Holetown, St. James parish. That evening we hung around the villa with my mom and Miss Cecilia, who drank rum punch and entertained us with stories about their prowess when they were young, single, and dating. Later, Hayes and I snuck out for dinner.

Friday I was awakened by the maid and asked to get ready to go boating. After the boat was docked, I found out we really weren't going boating. Instead, we were preparing to go snorkeling on a ten foot, two-passenger, inflatable boat, called the Rhino Rider. We spent the entire afternoon riding up and down the West Coast of Barbados, stopping to snorkel every now and again. I couldn't believe Hayes had so much energy for his age, but it worked for me. I shouldn't have been surprised because he watches what he eats and he works out three to four days a week.

According to Miss Cecilia, we got back to the villa just in time to get ready for dinner. She and Mom went along with us. It was only their second time leaving the house for a meal, which again proved to be a very entertaining and informative occasion for both myself and Hayes. As I got ready for bed I hoped Hayes would let me sleep in on Saturday, but no deal. He knocked on my door bright and early. This time he really did take me boating. Our one-day cruise on a catamaran took us to St. Lucia then to St. Vincent and the Grenadines. We also stopped and did some stargazing at the rich and famous on the island of Mustique. After that it was time to go home.

We got back after dark, but Hayes insisted we get dressed for dinner. He wanted to take me out on our last night in Barbados, which would allow us to end our last night with a blast.

"Mom, don't you think we should all do something together on our last night in Barbados?"

She shook her head adamantly. "No, Vada, you and Hayes go right ahead. Cecilia and I are going to drink a little more of this rum punch and just sit on the verandah and look out at the Caribbean."

Miss Cecilia added, "Oh, yes, Vada, I can't imagine spending my last night in Barbados any other way – unless, of course, you're going to allow me to spend some time alone with that Hayes. By the way, does he have any brothers? If his brothers are half as good as him, that's good enough for me."

"Miss Cecilia, I think you've had too much of that punch."

"Why, because I want to know if Hayes has any brothers; girl, I'm still a woman. It's been a long time, but I still know what to do."

"Both of his brothers are younger than him."

"If you can date an older man, surely I can date a younger one."

My mom and I laughed at Miss Cecilia's shenanigans. I think she has probably had too much rum the last four days, but to be honest, she wasn't much different when she was stone cold sober.

A chill went through my entire body as I watched Hayes come down the stairs. His brown skin had been darkened by the sun. He could have easily passed for a man in his early forties. He walked over to me and lightly kissed me on the lips.

"Barbados does you well. You're even more beautiful than usual," he whispered in my ear.

I shrugged my shoulders and chuckled. "So are you."

———

As we rode to the restaurant we talked about how quickly the last five days had gone by. He assured me we would be back soon. We only went a short distance down the West Coast to Derricks, St. James parish, stopping at the most spectacular restaurant we had eaten at during the entire trip, Carambola. It was perched on the side of a cliff, overlooking the Caribbean Sea. I didn't think it was possible to say that anything else in

Barbados was breathtaking, but it was. It was paradise. Hayes had called ahead and reserved a table on the patio.

He immediately ordered a bottle of champagne to celebrate our last night. He then thanked me for making the trip one of his most memorable trips ever. I thanked him for inviting me and my mom, and my mom's best friend. We drank champagne, laughed, talked, ate; drank a little more, laughed and talked a little more, and ate a little more. At the end of our meal Hayes insisted we have dessert, even after I told him I couldn't eat another bite. I asked him to choose something for me because no matter what he chose I would share it with him. He ordered a slice of bitter lemon cheesecake with apple gratin and black pepper burnt honey sauce.

When the cheese cake was served it looked so good I rolled my eyes because I knew there was no way I was going to be able to eat more than a couple of bites, even though I really wanted to. I took my fork and sliced a very small portion of it and placed it in my mouth. It was absolutely decadent. When I went to take my second bite, there was something in the garnish on the plate, so I picked at it with my fork. My eyes widened the size of quarters and my mouth became dry when I realized what it was, a beautiful, little tennis bracelet.

"Hayes, what is this? What is this?" I held it up in the air with my fork.

"I don't know, you tell me. What is it?"

I closed my eyes. "Oh, Hayes…you've already given me so much…this trip..."

"Are you going to be okay?"

"I don't know, give me a minute." I took a deep breath and used my napkin to clean the bracelet off.

The four carat, aquamarine stones, set in white gold, were beautiful. My hands were trembling so much Hayes had to reach across the table to help me put it on. I extended my right hand and nervously bounced in my seat as he secured the clasp.

"For a little over a year I've watched you and waited for the right time to say something to you. That morning in the elevator I felt like I had to strike while the iron was hot. I've pre-proposed to you already, so we're going to call this a pre-engagement gift." Hayes chuckled a little.

I fought the urge to go into a full-fledge, ugly cry. Instead, I got up and walked around the table and hugged him before excusing myself to go to the ladies room to pull myself together.

———

Back at the villa we walked the beach and talked. I found myself preoccupied with trying to figure out when Hayes would have had time to go shopping. Eventually, my curiosity got the best of me.

"We were together every day. How did you do it?"

He smiled. "What?"

"The bracelet…I mean, when did you have time?"

"I had help. Your mom and Cecilia picked it out while we were out on the catamaran today. I gave them the money and asked them to get something that said, 'there's more to come.'"

124

I playfully hit him on the shoulder. "I can't believe they were in on this with you. So, that's why they didn't want to come to dinner with us tonight."

He nodded his head. "They're probably waiting up for us too."

"When did y'all talk, when I was asleep?" I laughed at the idea of them plotting together.

"Basically…"

"I was joking, but y'all actually talked while I was sleeping? When…?"

We stopped walking. Hayes turned me around, pulled me close to his chest, and held me.

"Why do you need to know all of the details? Do you like the bracelet?"

"Of course, I love it. I think it's adorable that you did such a good job of surprising me."

As Hayes kissed me on the left side of my neck, I closed my eyes and breathed in the sea air.

"Then be quiet and let me make you happy. No more questions tonight. Okay?"

I purred in his arms.

He kissed me on my cheek…my forehead…the tip of my nose…and then softly brushed his lips back and forth across my lips before kissing me.

No more questions from me. We walked back to the house where my mom and Miss Cecilia were on the verandah waiting up for us. Neither of them was feeling any pain. Miss Cecilia got up and walked over and congratulated us, for what I wasn't sure.

"Vada, you could not have met a better man. Let me

see that beautiful bracelet."

I held my hand up as my mother got up from her seat and walked over to take a closer look.

Miss Cecilia stepped back and clasped her hands together. "When your mother and I were looking at all of that jewelry, I told her this man really loved you – giving you a pre-engagement gift." Tipsy and grinning ear to ear, Miss Cecilia clapped her hands.

Mother slurred, "Oh, Ce-cil."

Looking like she now remembered memories long gone, Ms. Cecilia agreed. "Okay, you're right. May I hug your fiancé, Vada? Hayes, come over here and let me get a hug. Have I told you how much I have enjoyed myself? The only thing that could have made this trip better is if I had brought my own man. Come on over here and let me hug you, Hayes."

A chorus of laughter echoed in the night air as Hayes walked over and gave her a hug.

Miss Cecilia thought we should all have a drink of rum punch to mark the occasion. I, on the other hand, thought we all should go to bed to get ready for our flight in the morning.

I looked over at my mom. "Mom, are you going to be okay? You and Miss Cecilia have been sucking those rum punches down all evening."

She didn't respond. Instead, she gave Hayes a kiss on the cheek and a hug good night, before turning to walk back into the house.

Sauntering over to Hayes, I also gave him a kiss on the cheek. "I'll see you bright and early in the morning.

Maybe we can have breakfast out by the pool before we leave?"

Hayes smiled at me adoringly. "That sounds like a nice idea. See you in the morning."

As I walked away, I grabbed his hand, and then the tips of his fingers, until our hands slipped apart. I walked upstairs with my mom and Miss Cecilia, while the two women sang a song they had learned during their stay in Barbados. In between their singing they talked on and on about my bracelet.

After walking into my bedroom, I closed the door behind me and immediately opened the doors to the balcony. I took a quick shower, slathered on lotion from head to toe, and sprayed on just a hint of perfume, before putting on some babydoll lingerie. I had come to the conclusion that before the night ended there should be one more surprise – for Hayes. I nervously sat out on the balcony contemplating what it would mean to cross this threshold in my relationship with Hayes, one I had never seriously considered crossing with anyone else. Each breath I took was quick and shallow. When his light went off in his room I knew I had to move quickly, before I changed my mind, or before he went to sleep.

I opened my bedroom door and before leaving my room, I looked down the hall at the bedroom door where my mom and Miss Cecilia were sleeping. I softly knocked on Hayes' door, as I slowly opened it and walked in. He immediately sat up in the bed. The bright moonlight shining through his open balcony doors illuminated his chiseled chest and enviable six-pack.

"Who is it? Is everything all right?" His voice sounded anxious and rushed.

"It's me, VJ." My voice cracked a little.

"Are you okay?"

I could see that he was squinting his eyes to see me.

"I couldn't sleep."

Instead of reaching for the light, he quickly stood up and walked over to meet me.

After reaching out and putting my arms around his neck, I softly kissed him on his lips. "I want you to make love to me."

His hands traveled up and down both sides of my body. "Vada…," he whispered.

I stopped him. "I want to do this…tonight."

His labored breaths fell heavily on my face as he pulled me closer. I knew he wanted me.

"Vada, baby, as much as I'd like to make love to you…and trust me…woo…I…woo…shoot, girl. I want you. I can't believe I'm saying this – it wouldn't be right."

As I looked up at his face, I could smell the soap from his shower. I trembled a little. "What do you mean it wouldn't be right?"

"You're a virgin…that's special, it's precious. You've waited 33 years." He struggled with his words. "I…can't begin to tell you…how difficult this is for me, but no… we're not going to make love tonight. I can't believe I'm saying this." He exhaled. "We're going to wait."

Shocked and blushing with embarrassment, I

attempted to pull away from him, but he held me tight.

"Why? We're going to get married. I mean, the bracelet tonight...everything felt right...I wanted to surprise you with something special...too." My face stung with humiliation.

"Vada, I do feel...this is special. The look on your face was priceless when you saw the bracelet. I can't tell you how it made me feel to see that I could make you that happy. I treasure the fact that you've never made love; that's a rarity these days. I feel privileged that I'll be your first... your only," he smiled. "I want it to be just like you've planned all of these years, with your husband, with me. If I was 22...shoot, if I was 32 or 42 we'd be rolling all over this bed right now, girl, but I'm 52. I've learned how to savor the good things. I want to treat you like the treasure you are. And please, don't think this is easy for me because it's not."

"I feel like a fool...coming in here." A single tear rolled down my cheek.

Using his finger, he wiped at my face. "No, please don't feel that way. Look, as difficult as this is for me; and trust me, this is very difficult..."

"You've said that already."

"Let me hold you while we just lie here together. Can we do that?"

I managed to give him an affirmative nod.

Hayes released me just long enough to adjust the pillows on his bed. After lying down he patted the bed next to him. "Come here."

I nuzzled up close to him, placing my head on his

bicep.

Jokingly, he whispered, "…and anyway, I don't want to make love to you for the first time with your mom and her drunken friend right next door." His muffled laughter filled the room.

With the sound of the waves in the background, Hayes kissed me on the forehead and held me. We lie together quietly until we both fell asleep. And so went our last night in sunny Barbados.

Chapter 13

June 14, 2012

We've been back in the States for almost two weeks. Hayes and I have lost our tans. Dee calls every time she's hears anything about me and Hayes. It seems that we're the "buzz" around the office. Folks were already talking, but after the trip to Barbados it really got crazy. I think some people are still trying to figure out if we were on vacation together. And everybody is trying to figure out who gave me my beautiful bracelet. It's kind of funny that Hayes and I are the ongoing topic of conversation around the office. It appears to do little more than amuse him.

Well, folks are really going to talk after tonight. Hayes and I are going to an attorney function together downtown. Even if we weren't dating each other, we would have both been there anyway. It'll be like "coming out" to our colleagues. Hayes should be pulling up any minute now.

THANKFUL FOR: coming out... ☺

 We pulled up to valet parking at the Omni Charlotte Hotel at 6:30 p.m. As Hayes opened the passenger door, I hesitantly exited the car. When we entered the ballroom it appeared things were just getting started.

Dinner was about to be served, so we quickly found our seats. Things jumped off quicker than I expected. As Hayes pulled out my chair a colleague walked up and gave him an overly nice hug, or so I thought.

"Please, let me introduce you. Vada, this is Helene Brookins of Brookins, Brookins & Stanley. Helene this is…"

"Let me guess, Vada Jade Bassett, an associate at your firm?" She turned and looked directly at me. "Please, it's not necessary to stand."

For a quick second I looked around the table to see who she might have been talking to. I heard my name come from her mouth, but I don't know what gave her the impression that I was going to stand to greet her.

"It's a pleasure to meet you, Helene." I attempted to offer a sincere smile, but the best I could do was a tight-lipped grin.

Helene gave Hayes another hug and walked back to her table, but not before inviting us to visit her table after dinner. We hadn't been there 15 minutes and I was ready to leave. Helene is a partner at one of the larger criminal defense practices in Charlotte, and she's known for being no nonsense and tough as nails. In other words, she is the consummate "B" word. The vibe I got from her wasn't a good one at all. It was also apparent that she wasn't happy with seeing me with Hayes. He, on the other hand, being a man, appeared oblivious to what was actually going on at that moment.

After dinner Hayes and I danced. I was able to learn something that I didn't know before – Hayes is a great dancer.

"You're pretty light on your feet."

"I can say the same for you, Ms. Bassett." He pulled me closer as he spoke.

"Thank you. So, when are we going to go dancing?"

Motioning as if he was about to twirl me around, he stopped short. "How about next weekend? You step?"

"Ooh, so you're telling me something else I didn't know – you're a big stepper, huh?"

"Sounds like you don't step…and I'm not one to brag, but, yes, I am a big stepper. I could probably teach you a thing or two."

"Do I hear a challenge? Do I?"

"Call it what you'd like…"

"Okay, don't back down now," I laughed.

Hayes pulled me closer, if that was even possible. "I never back down."

"You did in Barbados."

Why I said that I don't know, but I began to regret it the moment the words passed my lips. The music continued to play, but we stopped dancing.

Hayes looked down at me. "Is that what you really think, I backed down? I did that for you. I don't think you appreciate what you were asking for that night. Making love will change our relationship. It'll create certain expectations…unwarranted urgency. I don't have to 'back down' again. If that's what you'd like. I'm up for that challenge, as well."

After having said all that he had to say he gave me a lingering kiss on the cheek and began dancing again, just as the music ended. I discretely glanced around the room to see if anyone had noticed us talking. Helene Brookins was walking in our direction, so I suddenly had an urge to go to the ladies' room. I didn't feel like being a part of the show that she was about to put on.

I nervously smiled at Hayes. "Do you mind, I need to excuse myself for just a moment. I won't be long."

Hayes' eyes searched my face. "You better not be."

As I walked away, I could hear Helene's annoying voice calling Hayes' name. I turned and looked back just as she was raising her arms to embrace him. He's the quintessential gentleman, so he would certainly give her another hug. She wasn't the kind of woman Hayes wanted – overbearing and arrogant. I had heard rumors about her that weren't so flattering, and Hayes was discrete and private. He wouldn't want someone whose business was in the streets. That was one thing I was pretty sure of. I had also heard, through the legal grapevine, that Helene had been married three times, and possibly more.

When I returned to the ballroom Hayes motioned for me to come over to Helene's table. It looked like she and her entourage had been drinking a lot, something that I hadn't noticed before. There was quite a bit of laughter and commotion at her table, and I really didn't feel like matching wits with her. I was there to have a good time with Hayes. As I approached, Hayes stood and placed his arm around my waist. That was better than I had even hoped for. He was making it clear that we were a couple. Helene cut her eyes at me, but continued to laugh and talk. She continued to ask us to join her at her table, but Hayes declined.

"Thanks, Helene, but VJ and I have another engagement, so we're actually going to be leaving soon."

Helene continued to wear a plastic smile, though she looked at me as if she was going to get up and grab me by my throat and lift me off of my feet.

"Oh, Hayes, don't be silly. You and Ms. Bassett have plenty of time for that. You have all night, as a matter of fact." She patted the chair next to her. "Here, sit down and join us for just a little while. It won't be quite like old times, but I'm sure you both will enjoy yourselves."

Hayes grabbed Helene's hand and kissed it. "Thanks again for the invitation, Helene, but we really have to leave." Hayes looked over at me. "…unless you'd like to stay a little while longer?"

I smiled at him and defiantly glanced at Helene, before looking back at Hayes. "No, I think we should go on to our next engagement."

"Well, folks, the lady has spoken. Please enjoy the rest of your evening."

With that, we turned and walked away.

After just a few feet, Hayes grabbed my hand and kissed it. "I didn't want you to be jealous because I kissed ole' Helene's hand. You know that was just a friendly gesture, right?"

I nodded my head. "Now, what is this other engagement we have?"

Hayes laughed. "You know, earlier it crossed my

mind to ask you if you wanted to go someplace else after dinner…since we're all dressed up. When Helene became so persistent, I thought the best thing for us to do was to leave before she had that one drink that always takes her over the edge. If there's no place in particular that you'd like to go, I was thinking we could go to this little jazz joint that I like, The Jazz Gallery."

"Sounds like a plan. Let's do it."

We hung out at the Gallery until it closed. On the way home we talked about Salsa dancing next time...my thing.

————

The next morning I called Dee, mostly to tell her about Helene. "Hey, girl, I know it's early for you, get up anyway."

Dee sounded groggy, but pleasant. "What's up? How was last night?"

"It was great, except for Helene Brookins. If we had been in high school I'm pretty sure she would have fought me over Hayes."

With the mention of Helene Brookins' name, I had sparked Dee's interest.

"Let me sit up and get comfortable." I could hear the rustling of covers in the background. "Okay, you have my full attention now. So, Helene was there? I hear that chick's a witch, and that's on a good day. I don't know her well enough to say for sure. I know I can't stand her." Dee laughed. "I've heard lots of things about her and I've had the pleasure of seeing her from afar several times. To tell you the truth, I think that was enough for me. So tell me, what happened?"

"It wasn't much, just enough. I don't know if I'm prepared to fight these older chicks for Hayes."

Wanting to hear only the juicy parts, Dee goaded me on. "Unh, huh…what happened?"

I wanted to tell the story the way I wanted to tell it, as well as tease Dee, so I continued. "Could you show a little bit of sensitivity, please?"

"VJ?"

"What?"

"What do I have to do to get you tell me what happened with Brookins?"

I laughed. "Anyway…she came over to our table to speak to Hayes. It was this whole production. Hayes didn't really have a chance to introduce me before she interrupted him and said I must be an associate from the firm. And check this out. Then she tells me it's not necessary for me to stand, to greet her. Can you believe that?"

"From the things I've heard about her, sounds like she was gentle with you. I'm sure that had nothing to do with you though. She probably didn't want to let her fangs show in front of Hayes. He's kind of no nonsense and I'm sure she's more than aware that there's certain behavior that he completely disapproves of. Girl, you know that couldn't have been me. You were probably really nice about the whole thing. I admire your patience and tolerance for that kind of foolishness. I'm sure all of that will change after you have kids. Okay, go ahead with the rest of the story. There's got to be more."

"Dee, you were like you are long before you had Quincy."

She had to laugh because it was true. "Stop trying to change the subject. This isn't about me."

"Oh, my bad, okay, so later when we were dancing; actually, we had just finished dancing, so I excused myself to go to the ladies' room. I look back, and guess who I see coming out on the dance floor?"

I could tell I really had Dee's attention now.

"…to do what?"

"I don't know if she was asking Hayes to dance or what, I just kept walking."

"See…"

"See what?"

"I would have been all over her."

"Anyway, I come back and Hayes is standing at her table. She's begging him to join her and her party. It's obvious she's had a lot to drink, but girlfriend was not the slightest bit ashamed of her begging. She did everything except pull up her dress and bend over the table."

Dee tentatively continued her line of questioning. "So, you think she and Hayes have done that 'thang' before or did you not ask him?"

"Of course I didn't ask him that?"

Dee smacked her lips. "Again, the difference between me and you; I would have asked him what her problem was and I would have wanted to know if they'd ever had sex."

I was prepared to go head to head with my friend to defend Hayes.

"I don't know that he has been…."

"He's a man, isn't he?"

"So, what is that supposed to mean?"

"There's a far greater chance that he's been with someone since his wife's death than there is that you will be with anybody before you get married."

"Does everything always have to be about sex with you?"

"I didn't make the rules. I just apply them. So, don't get upset with me because you don't know the rules. I'm really surprised that Hayes hasn't tried to…" She cleared her throat. "…make love to you."

Now I was annoyed and hated that I had even bothered to call Dee. I had become the student, as so often is the case in these kinds of conversations with her.

"Why do the rules say he should have tried by now?"

"Again, he's a man, isn't he?"

"Well, I hate to sound so uninformed…"

"You can't help it, honey…and I don't even hold it against you."

"Don't interrupt me again, Dee. Like I was saying, I don't get the feeling Hayes is typical. When we were in Barbados…I went to his room …"

Dee sounded like she had jumped to her feet. She excitedly raised her voice. "You have been holding out. What kind of friend are you? You know I always want to know the juice."

"Didn't I tell you not to interrupt me? I'm not going

to tell you again."

"Okay, okay, continue."

"Now I have to start from the beginning. Barbados was amazing. Dee, it's so beautiful. That's why I called you and told you that you and your people need to plan a vacation there. Every day that I was there, I don't know; I either wanted to or felt like I had to make love to Hayes. So, one night after we got back to the house I put on this sexy little babydoll thing I had brought with me… and I went to his room."

Dee gasped.

"What was that?"

"Nothing, I think I'm about to hyperventilate. Why did you have a 'sexy little thing' in your suitcase? I'm just asking, but go on."

"Well, I went to his room and I told him I wanted to make love."

"What happened? What did he say?"

"He said no."

"What the… He told you no? Is he, uhm, I can't think of the word right now, but you know what I'm talking about. He can't do the thing?"

"No, it was nothing like that. He told me it was special that I was a virgin…that he didn't want to ruin that for me…that he wanted us to wait…until we got married."

"That negro is fairytale sweet. If it wasn't you telling me this story I would call you a liar and tell you he's running game on you. What's his name said the same thing and look at what he was doing – screwing somebody else, probably everybody else. Still, in some circles they would call Hayes, let's see, crazy? I can't believe he didn't take advantage of that opportunity: romantic island, virgin girl, sexy lingerie…girl, I would have taken advantage of you with all of that going on."

"Oh, it doesn't end there. After he said no, he asked me if he could just hold me. So, that's how we slept."

"Girl, stop trying to make me cry. Do you hear me? I'm just going to tell myself that he's impotent because I know he's not gay. That's the word I was looking for earlier, impotent. All jokes aside, though, he…is not real. Can't be…ain't no way."

"Dee, hold on for a minute. Somebody else is calling."

I quickly clicked over to answer the other call.

"Hello."

"Sweetie, this is your dad."

He was the last person I expected to hear from so early on a Saturday morning. "Oh, hi, Daddy, hold on for a minute. I need to get Dee off of the other line."

I clicked back over. "Dee, guess who that is on my other line?"

Frowning, Dee said the first name that entered her mind. "I know it's not that doggish William."

"No, it's my dad."

"Well, that's good. I'll talk with you later. Tell Daddy Bassett I said hello."

———

Annoyed, but glad to hear from my father, I clicked

back over to him. "What's up, Daddy? To what do I owe this pleasure?"

"Do I need a special reason to call you now?"

"Uh, uh…"

"Well, how are you? Are you still mad with me?"

"I'm fine. As far as being mad with you is concerned, I don't know if I'm mad or not. I'm still adjusting to everything."

"That's basically why I'm calling. I'd like to invite you and William over for dinner."

My first response should have probably been to tell him that I wasn't dating William anymore; that I, in fact, had not even talked with William in months now.

"Dinner, huh, when?"

"Tonight, if you're free."

"Why such short notice, Daddy?"

"LaDonna and I have been talking about this for a while, and I think it's time you both met. You and she are, after all, family now."

I took a deep breath and made a very weak attempt to refrain from sounding sarcastic. I shook my head before responding because I couldn't believe her referred to us as family.

"I take it LaDonna is Monyet's mother?"

"Of course she is, sweetie."

Biting my bottom lip, I found myself flustered and, for a brief moment, words escaped me.

"Uhh…"

"VJ, are you still there, honey?"

"Yeah, I'm here."

"What about tonight? Do you think you and William can make it tonight?"

"Sure, Daddy, I don't know why not. We have to get this over with at some point."

My dad sounded exhausted, probably more so from the conversation that preceded his dinner invitation to me than from our actual conversation. If he thought asking me to come to dinner tired him out, he was in for a rude awakening.

"Let me get something to write with so you can give me your address.

————

Hayes and I pulled into the driveway of a professionally landscaped yard. I took note of the fact that the house was bigger than the one my mother lived in. Parked in the driveway was my dad's big, old, pewter Mercedes E-Class and right next to it was a beautiful baby blue, convertible BMW. Hayes pulled up behind both cars and put the car in park before turning it off.

After taking the key out of the ignition, he turned and looked at me. "You haven't said much. Are you all right?"

Making an attempt to sound positive, I looked over at him and gave him a closed lip smile. "Yep, I suppose I'm okay; just a little anxious. I can't believe I'm here to visit my dad and his girlfriend. How crazy is that?"

"VJ, I promise you, it's not going to be as bad as you've built it up to be. Who knows, you might like this woman."

"Okay, if you say so. By the way, I didn't tell my dad you were coming. He's expecting William."

Frowning with disapproval, Hayes struggled to maintain his composure. "Why didn't you tell him about me?"

"Probably…I don't know. He's introducing me to his new wife, I guess I wanted to have someone new to introduce too."

Hayes looked at me, shook his head, and got out of the car. After walking around to my side, he opened my door and smiled as he held it open for me.

"You could step back and give me a little room to get out."

Grabbing me by the hand, he pulled me from the car. Holding me close to his chest, he gave me a hug before kissing me on the forehead. "Now, is that a little better? You know you needed that, right?"

I smiled, even though I was ashamed that he was seeing such a childish side of me.

I stood on my tiptoes and kissed him on the lips. "Thanks for the hug, but that's what I really needed."

"Come on before your dad looks out the window and sees us out here kissing. I don't think any good would come from that. It wouldn't be a good look if I was my daughter's boyfriend."

"Okay, how crazy did that sound?" I chuckled. "Careful, you're slipping into my silly little world."

"You know what I mean. Come on, let's go to the door."

———

Right from the start, I realized dinner was a mistake. After hugging me, my dad introduced me to LaDonna, who motioned as if to hug me too. Too familiar, far too quickly for me, so I extended my hand, instead. I sensed my dad's disappointment, but thought: *Give me a break; this is only the woman that you left my mother for.* Hayes was nice and on point. He introduced himself to my dad and LaDonna, and being the gentleman that he is, he shook my dad's hand and kissed Miss LaDonna on the cheek.

Our mean was actually delicious. Not memorable, but delicious. My dad attempted to give me and LaDonna some alone time, by suggesting that we clear the table while he and Hayes went into the other room to talk. Hayes obviously read the look on my face and offered to carry some of the dishes into the kitchen. He cornered me in the hallway.

"You could be a little nicer because it's obvious that your dad is trying very hard to make the situation as pleasant as possible."

I looked up at him, but didn't bother to respond. I knew he was right, but not only was Monyet present during dinner, but so was her brand, spanking, new baby brother. Monyet was quite proud of him too. My dad had failed to mention the baby, Mansel Lawrence Bassett, Jr. I felt vindicated with my decision not to tell him about Hayes. Again, hurt and disappointed by the most important man in my life. My dad had a new wife, a new family, and a new life. I could hardly wait to leave.

Dad and Hayes seemed to have a great deal to talk about. It really wasn't a surprise; they're pretty close in age. I could say the same for myself and LaDonna. I was sure my dad's new wife wasn't much older than me. Unlike my dad and Hayes, LaDonna and I had very little to say to each other, though. I had come to the conclusion that she had those babies so quickly because she wanted to lock herself into his money. As far as I was concerned, the evening couldn't end fast enough.

As Hayes and I prepared to leave, I hugged my dad and gave his wife a two-handed handshake: the kind where you cup the other person's hand in between both of yours. That was my inconsiderate attempt to show a little warmth. I thanked her for dinner and told her I was sure we'd see each other again, soon. Hayes, again, shook my dad's hand, kissed the wife on the cheek, and thanked them both for the lovely dinner, and for having him over. Out of nowhere, Monyet came running over and hugged my leg. It was all I could do to keep from breaking down and crying right there in front of everybody.

In the car on the way home, Hayes attempted to make small talk, but there was absolutely nothing that I wanted to talk about. Once we arrived back at my house we sat hugged up on the couch as we watched a movie, until I told him I thought I would call it a night.

Before getting up he sat forward and looked over at me. "VJ, I know this has to be difficult for you, but I promise you, you'll get passed this. If you'd like, I can stay tonight?"

"Hmph…thanks, but that's okay. I just want to be alone. And anyway, I'm tired. I really just want to go to bed."

"Okay. Call me if you need to talk. I'm a good listener."

"I know…" I hugged him hard.

Hayes kissed me on the forehead before nudging my chin up and kissing me on the lips. As we kissed I thought: *…and I get to have this forever and ever, Amen.*

"You sure you don't want me to stay?"

I stood up and pulled him up to his feet. "Yep, I'm sure. I'll be okay. Nothing a good night's sleep won't fix."

I walked him to the door then cried as I watched him back down the driveway.

The next morning my phone rang as I walked in from the gym. "Hello."

"Vada, it's your dad."

"Hey, Daddy, what's up?"

"I'm calling to let you know that I'm very disappointed by the way you acted last night."

His words caught me off guard.

"Excuse me?"

"You know exactly what I'm talking about. LaDonna's feelings were hurt because you blew her off most of the night. You were actually very rude and disrespectful."

"LaDonna's feelings were hurt? Pardon me if I don't

buddy up with your mistress. The only thing she and I have in common is you. So, let's not get things twisted, Daddy. I don't want to hear about her feelings being hurt. She's not the only one with hurt feelings in this soap opera. So, again, pardon me if I don't care about her feelings. I bet her feelings weren't hurt when she was seeing you behind my mother's back or while she was making those babies for you? Daddy, trust me, you don't even want to go there with me."

"Look, Vada, LaDonna and I are together, so you're just going to have to get used to it."

"Actually, I don't have to get used to anything. She's nothing to me. If anything, she would have been more in line if she were one of my protégés. She and I are about the same age; correct?"

"...and Hayes isn't my age? What happened to William?"

"I haven't seen or talked with William in months, and I don't think now's the time for you to be getting overly sensitive about age. Age didn't seem to be an issue when you began your affair with LaDonna. Oh, and uh, if you hadn't alienated me and moved on with your 'new' life, you would have known that William and I broke up."

"Vada are you trying to hurt me by dating someone old enough to be your father?"

"My dating Hayes has nothing to do with you...and who are you to tell me who I can and cannot date?"

"I'm your father!"

"And..."

"What do you mean and? What's wrong with you?"

"It seems to me that you have your hands full being the father to all of those babies you've made with your new wife, which, I think, is absolutely ridiculous. Those should be my children."

"Well, I don't think you have to worry about having children any time soon. What's his name? Hayes...probably has children and grandchildren."

"Excuse me for pointing out the obvious, but you're older than him and that didn't stop you from having more children. Daddy, if you called here to argue with me, you've succeeded. You've actually done a superb job, but you know what? I don't care to continue this conversation."

"Vada, I think you owe me...and LaDonna an apology."

"Hmph...tell her to wait on it. I'm hanging up now. Bye, Daddy..."

When the phone rang again I knew it was my dad calling back. Teary-eyed, I stubbornly stood by and looked at the phone. My dad and I have never argued like that before. Even when I was a teenager, we never went at each other's throats like that. I wanted the daddy I knew back.

I called Dee as quickly as my fingers could press the buttons. I didn't say hello or give her time to say much else.

"Dee, I just hung up on my dad."

"What's wrong? What happened? Did something happen last night during dinner?"

"Oh, that's right; I didn't tell you about dinner, did I?

He called me because he wanted me to apologize to his 'LaDonna.'"

"What do you mean apologize? What really happened last night?"

"I thought I was on my best behavior, under the circumstances. I might have been a little distant, okay, and a little cold, but that's about it. My dad wanted us to be one great, big ole happy family. And Dee, you know that's not going to happen. You know me. You know I wouldn't purposely disrespect my dad or that woman. Oh, and as far as the baby…"

"Monyet?

"Oh, nooo, the new baby!"

"New baby? What new baby? How many more children has your dad had?"

"Check this out. The baby's name is Mansel Lawrence, Jr."

"Oh, man, and a junior to boot; how's that for the proverbial 'cherry' on top?"

"Girl, as far as I'm concerned, this is just one big mess. I told my dad those should be my children; the man is having his own grandchildren. Then he had the nerve to tell me that having children should be my least concern because he knows Hayes must have his own children, as well as his own grandchildren."

"Sounds like y'all both probably threw a few low blows. Other than that, what did your dad think about Hayes?"

"Honestly, he seemed to like him…a lot."

"Like I said, y'all were both throwing low blows, but

I'm sure some of your dad's were because he was nervous. He was probably nervous about you meeting the other chick, the other babies, and whatever."

"You're right, whatever. What else has he not told me?"

"Girl, there's not much else he can pull from his hat, at this point. Look, tell me, what did his jump off look like? She must be all that, and then some, to break up a family."

"Actually, she was just average – short, light-skinned, big hips, big breasts, long hair. She was kind of thick, but that could have been baby weight."

"And what did the doggone house look like?"

"First of all, it's over in that new subdivision, Meadow Lawn."

"Ooh, snap, big house, huh?"

"That's an understatement."

————

June 16, 2012

It's about 10:30 at night and I've managed to avoid talking to everyone today, except my dad and Dee. It's not because I haven't received any other calls. My mom called and left a message telling me my dad had called her because he was really upset. She wanted me to call her as soon as I received her message. Dee called back to see if I wanted to do anything. Hayes called to tell me he missed me and he was hoping we could have dinner. I didn't feel like being bothered with anybody. I didn't have the energy. I feel like I don't know that man – my dad – anymore. "LaDonna's feelings were hurt?" Forget LaDonna, who does she think she is? Did she think we were going to be friends? That we would all be adults about the situation and that I would ignore the fact that she and my dad had an affair, while he was married to my mother, and had, not one, but two children. I wonder what my daddy said to my mom when he called her…to tell on me. How about that for the shoe being on the other foot! My dad is calling my mom about me. My mom used to be the one threatening to tell my dad when I did something wrong. "Mansel won't believe his only child is acting like this. Wait until I tell him how you've been behaving." And the fact that he's calling her because he didn't like the way I was treating his jump off. Who'd a thought life would become so complicated? I guess I better call my mother back…tomorrow. If I don't, she'll come over and I don't think I want to deal with her face-to-face right now.

I'm going to work from home tomorrow and Tuesday. I think I might go in for a half-day Wednesday and Thursday, and work from home on Friday. If I hadn't just got back from vacation with Hayes I'd take the entire week off. I just don't feel like being bothered with anything or anybody.

I'm going to bed. I'm sick and tired of being sad and definitely sick and tired of being sick and tired…

THANKFUL FOR: a place to lie my head

Chapter 14

Hayes called first thing Monday morning.

I stretched, and then answered the phone. "Hel-lo…"

"Are you still in the bed? VJ, is everything okay?"

"What time is it?"

"It's 8 o'clock. You should be on your way to work. What's going on with you?"

"I'm working from home today."

"Why, are you not feeling well? I called you yesterday. If you had called me back I would have come over to take care of you."

"I'm okay."

"You're not still pouting about dinner with your dad are you?"

"I didn't realize I was pouting." I sat up in my bed. "Is that what you think I'm doing, pouting?"

"A little, but it's okay. It's your father. You'll get over it in time, sort of like my daughter feels about you. When I first started seeing you she pouted for a while, but she seems to have worked it out. I think she's finally convinced that you don't have any intention of hurting her daddy. I don't know if you've forgotten, but, for what it's worth, you're significantly younger than me."

His words were like a never-ending, broken tape.

I chose not to acknowledge what he said. "I had a really bad argument with my dad yesterday."

"How bad?"

"Really bad. He doesn't care for me seeing you

because you're his age and he thinks I owe his wife an apology for the way I treated her. You know, just a bunch of foolishness."

"Look, I can't tell you how to deal with your dad, no more than I can tell your dad how to deal with you regarding your family matters, but I do know that y'all have to work this out at some point. Your mom seems to have things under control; and, VJ, there are so many other things to consider, other than yourself. There are small children involved, this other woman, your mom, and your dad. I know he loves you, and you know he loves you, but people make mistakes. I mean, unfortunately, that's life. Surely you understand that. At some point you either forgive them or you don't, but you have to go on. Look, I'm not by far an expert on this. I have skeletons in my closet just like everybody else. I guess what I'm saying is, you need to go talk with someone, a professional perhaps. After my wife died I had some trouble getting past her death. I eventually had to go talk with somebody about it. What you're dealing with is a death of sorts. If I give you the doctor's name and number will you at least give her a call?"

"Hayes…"

"VJ, promise me you'll call her. I hate to see you like this. You need to work things out with your father because you're allowing what's going on with him to impact our relationship and that's not's working, for me. The doctor's name is Dr. Hanyard. I'll give you her number. Promise me you'll call her…today."

"Okayyy, I promise. I'll call her."

"Call me after you talk with her."

"What is this now? You don't think I'm going to call her?"

"Of course I do. I just want to talk with you after you've talked with her. No big deal. I'm preparing for a trial next week, so if Helen says I'm not available when you call, just tell her I said to interrupt me. If I see her when I get to the office, I'll also let her know I'm expecting your call."

"You're not afraid to tell her that?" A smile glided across my face.

"I don't think we're that much of a secret anymore. She probably still thinks you're too young, but she'll just have to deal with it. Aside from that, I'm sure she approves of you." He chuckled at the idea of being approved by his secretary.

"Well, that's good to know."

"Okay, let's hang up so you can give Dr. Hanyard a call."

"I love the way you take care of me, Hayes. Thank you."

———

Before getting out of the car I pondered over the things Hayes said earlier. *He's right; I need to work things out with my dad. Actually, I need to work things out with myself. The major players in this scenario, my mom and dad, seem to be emotionally intact and moving on with their respective lives. What's my problem? Why can't I move past this hurdle?* I sighed heavily as I walked into the doctor's office. With so many more important things going on in the world, here I was visiting a psychologist because I couldn't work out my daddy issues.

The office was gorgeous, very comfortable and homey; the receptionist very approachable. I smiled when I thought about how much the young lady looked like Angie Stone, afro and all.

She kindly handed me a questionnaire attached to a clipboard and asked me to fill it out. "Dr. Hanyard will be with you in just a few minutes."

"Thank you."

After completing the questionnaire, and giving it back to the receptionist, I looked around for a magazine to browse through while I waited: Jet, Ebony, Essence, Shape, People, Parent & Child, Men's Health, Esquire, Sports Illustrated, Cosmopolitan, GQ, Town & Country, "O," and an assortment of children magazines – *quiet a hodge-podge of literature.* Before I could get involved in the "O" magazine that I had picked up, a door to my right opened. A young boy, his mother, and another motherly looking, older woman exited. The older woman hugged the little boy and his mother and told them she would see them next week. She then directed her attention to me.

With her right hand extended she introduced herself. "Hello, Vada Bassett? I'm Dr. Hanyard. I hope I didn't keep you waiting very long?"

I stood and shook her hand. "Not at all, I appreciate you allowing me to come in on such short notice."

Holding the door open, the doctor directed me to an inner hallway.

"Well, one person's cancellation is another person's appointment." She gently brushed her hand against my shoulder and nodded her head to the left to further guide me in the right direction. "My office is around the corner and to the left."

Her smile was closed lipped, but very warm; her voice, strangely soothing and reassuring. With her graying locs swept up away from her face, it was easy to see how attractive she was.

"Ms. Bassett, please have a seat anywhere you might feel comfortable. I'm going to sit over here." She gestured, pointing at a comfortable overstuffed chair for herself.

I chose to take a seat on one end of the large, equally overstuffed couch. When I first walked into the doctor's office I was very surprised by the Boho decor. In addition to several large and small plants throughout the room, there were also a few candles strategically placed. On the mantle were photos of her family. I was pretty sure it was her family because there was a bulletin board, hanging to the left of the mirror, which had, what looked like, hundreds of pictures of other people on it. My reverie was eventually disrupted by the doctor's voice.

"So, Ms. Bassett, let me tell you a little about myself. Well, you know my name, Dorothy Hanyard. My friends and colleagues call me Dot. I'm 67 years old. I've been married for 38 years to the same man, I might add. I have four children, two boys and two girls; there ages are 35, 32, 28, and 25; my oldest and my youngest are girls. No grandchildren yet, but I'm eagerly awaiting their arrival."

I laughed. "Where'd that 25 year old come from?"

The doctor gave me a broad, toothy grin. "Your guess is as good as mine. I don't know what I was thinking when that happened, but she's a beautiful, intelligent, young lady. I can't even imagine life without her."

"That's beautiful."

"And true, but, of course, only after we made it through those dreaded teenage years." The doctor laughed as if she had told a joke. "Let me finish telling you about myself, so we can talk about you. I have a B.S. in Social Studies, a Master's degree in Psychology, and a Ph.D. in Family Sciences; and I've been practicing for, uhm, about thirty years."

"Wow, quite impressive."

"Glad to hear that you think so. Now, tell me a little about yourself."

"Where should I begin? I'm 33 years old. I'm an only child. I'm an attorney at Allen, Vishmell & Taylor. Let's see, what else? Oh, I've never been married. I'm a virgin…"

"Really? That's pretty interesting. Don't you think?"

"I guess. You tell me, you're the doctor."

We both laughed.

"I do a lot of volunteer work, particularly with children. I enjoy writing poetry. I've kept a journal since, probably, the first time I could write. I read, on average, about four books a month…and I can't think of anything else right now."

"Well, that was pretty good. If you think of anything else that you'd like to share with me, feel free to share it at any time. How did I come to have the pleasure of making your acquaintance?"

"Uhm, Hayes Vishmell."

"Oh, Hayes…he is a really wonderful person isn't he? How is he?"

"He's doing well."

"So, you're a friend of his daughter?"

"No, I actually just met his daughter a few weeks ago."

"Yes, you did say you worked as an attorney at Allen, Vishmell & Taylor. So, you work together?"

"I suppose, to some degree, yes…and we're seeing each other."

The doctor didn't immediately respond, but she seemed to write quite a few notes on her legal pad. I sat up and stretched my neck to peek at what she was scribbling.

"Was that a bad answer?"

"No, no, no…not at all. There are no bad or wrong answers in the confines of these walls."

"Ohhh…"

"Okay, now, what brought you in today to talk with me?"

"I'm almost embarrassed to say."

"You shouldn't be. I'm not here to criticize or judge you. I'm basically here to listen."

"You make a lot of money to do that, huh?"

"You make a lot of money to do what you do too, don't you?

"Touché doctor, I guess I'm here because my dad divorced my mother."

"Okay, here is where I ask one of those questions that make me appear really intelligent. So, how do you feel about that, your dad divorcing your mother?"

"Well, Dr. Hanyard, I guess how I feel is the reason why I'm here. I'm angry, disappointed, sad, disgruntled, confused, you name it; and I just don't know how to make sense of it or how to put it behind me. My dad is obviously a part of the fabric of my life, but these days I'm feeling like that fabric has been ripped."

"That was a great analogy. Do you mind if I use it sometime?"

"Sure, it was a spontaneous thought. I think."

"Well, I thought I better ask because you know how some attorney types are, copyrights, intellectual property, etc."

We both laughed. I really like her sense of humor.

"I'm sorry. I didn't mean to get off track. How long were your parents married and how long have they been divorced? And, please, feel free to use the Kleenex on the table there if you feel you need to." She pointed and nodded her head as she gestured towards the end table to my left.

"Thank you," was all I managed to say, as my eyes filled with tears. "My dad told me in March that he was moving out and that he and my mom were getting a divorce, so the divorce was probably final in May. They had been married for 40 years."

The doctor's brow rose. "That's a long time. I can see why you're upset." She continued to fervently write on her notepad. "What was the reason he gave you for filing for divorce? I assume it was your father that initiated the divorce."

"Yes, it was. I suppose it was because he was seeing another woman. He said his reason for divorcing my mom was because, I think, he said it was because people change, or he didn't feel needed. I don't know, but whatever the reason was that he gave me, it was absolutely ridiculous."

"Are there any other children involved?"

"Yep, two…"

"How did you find out about the children?"

"Oh, my dad invited me to lunch and there was Monyet. And just the other night he invited me over for dinner to meet this other woman and, what do you know, there was a little baby there too."

"Okay, so he has remarried and I take it he didn't tell you about either of the children prior to you meeting them?"

"Nope…and I don't think he's married to her yet." I reached for the Kleenex as a tear trickled down my cheek.

"Why does that make you cry?"

As I wiped at my eyes and my nose, my chin began to tremble. "Because…" I took a breath. "…I can't believe I'm crying."

"Why not, Vada; may I call you Vada? Please feel

free to call me Dot."

"By all means, please call me Vada or VJ, but I'll be calling you Dr. Hanyard."

The doctor seemed to smile approvingly with her eyes. "Why is it hard for you to believe you're crying?"

"I'm 33 years old…"

"…and your father has been there with you for those 33 years, so it can be a little difficult to accept that kind of change after so many years. Then you have the added nuance of finding out that you now have a stepmother, of sorts, and younger siblings. That has to be terribly painful. You might feel a little displaced, a little resentful?"

I chuckled. "That's exactly what I felt…feel. I can't believe that he would just thrust these children on me like he did. The same way he told me about the divorce. He just did it; no forewarning or anything."

"Why did that surprise you so much? Was that out of character for him?"

"Oh, definitely; we've always talked about everything – I mean everything. I'm like the son he never had. He talked to me about dating, about how I should be treated by boys, and when I grew up, men; about sex; you name it. He even insisted that he be there when my mom talked to me about my menstrual cycle. He never shied away from talking with me about anything. I mean anything – even if it made him uncomfortable."

"Okay, so you're a little confused by his recent behavior, not talking to you regarding this whole situation?"

"I never thought about it before, but yeah, I guess I am. I think I would feel just a little bit better about all of this if we had just sat down and talked about it, instead of him springing things on me, one at a time, like he's been doing. And then yesterday, we had the biggest argument that we have ever had. It was off the charts. I have never spoken to my father like I did yesterday. I ended the conversation by politely hanging up the phone on him; if there's a polite way to hang up on someone. I was so disrespectful, but I couldn't stop myself."

"So, regarding that particular conversation, nothing was resolved I take it?"

"Less than nothing was resolved. He wanted me to apologize because he thought I was rude and disrespectful to her the night before."

"Were you?"

"Dr. Hanyard, honestly, I don't think I was. I was probably more apprehensive and taken aback than anything else. I'm visiting my dad and this woman in their home, not far from where my mom lives."

"Excuse me, I don't mean to interrupt, but what's this woman's name?"

"I'm sorry. Her name is LaDonna."

"Okay, LaDonna." Dr. Hanyard took a quick note. "Okay, I'm sorry, continue."

"Okay, let's see. Where was I? Oh, as if it wasn't enough that I was meeting...LaDonna, then I find out they have a new baby, in addition to the other child, both of whom, by the way, had to be conceived while he was still married to my mother. I think there were more prevailing issues there for me than making his…LaDonna feel welcome. In addition to that, he was also upset because I brought Hayes with me and, as you know, Hayes is a few years older than me. So my dad thinks it's totally inappropriate for me to date him. How hypocritical is that? I don't think my dad should be throwing stones, since he's living in a great big ole' glass house. So, doctor, that's where I am, and that's why I'm sitting here talking to you today. Hayes thought I needed to work this out sooner rather than later."

"Well, Vada, he's absolutely correct. Sooner is always better than later, but later is definitely better than never. We'd hate for this to…" She paused. "…trickle down to other relationships in your life. I would say that we have quite a bit to work with here. May I ask you a question before we go on?"

"Of course…"

"Is there any particular reason why you began dating Hayes at this time in your life?"

I pursed my lips and carefully considered the doctor's question before responding. "Honestly, no. My previous relationship ended and Hayes approached me. We realized there was a mutual attraction, and one thing led to another."

"Hmph…okay." The doctor, again, wrote notes on her legal pad. "This is a good place for us to end today. I'd like for you to think about some things for our next visit. You referred to your life now as being like 'ripped fabric.' Next time we meet I'd like to talk a little further about your relationship with your father and your mother as part of that fabric. I'd also like to discuss the different ways you feel that fabric has actually been ripped. Then we can go from there – establishing goals to repair that rip, so to speak. I'd also like to consider how your relationship with Hayes fits into all of this. How does that sound?"

"Sounds pretty good to me, doctor."

"You think so? Well, it gets even better. Wait until your third or fourth visit!"

We both laughed.

"Now, I typically see my clients once a week, unless more frequent visits are warranted. How often would you like to come in?"

"To be honest with you, I'd rather not wait a week. Can I come back on Friday?" I looked away and pulled my Day-Timer from my purse.

Moving to her desk to look at her calendar, Dr. Hanyard cocked her head to one side. "Hmmmm, let's see, I think I can squeeze you in Friday."

I pulled out a pen to write down the time. "Friday anytime is good for me. I can make myself available. Since we're looking at the calendar, is it okay if I go ahead and confirm some other dates, as well?"

"That's a really good idea. My calendar fills up very quickly. I can slip you in very early or very late on Wednesday or Thursday of next week. I'm going out of town for the holiday, so I'm not going to be available July 5th through the 8th. My husband and I are going on an abbreviated vacation, but I will be back in the office on Monday, July 9th. Let's see. I have an opening at 10 o'clock the morning of the 10th. Will that work for you?"

By the time we finished I had appointments for twice a week, for the remainder of the month of June and for the entire month of July. Dr. Hanyard formidably accommodated my need to talk to make sense of the things going on in my life. I hadn't even left the doctor's office before I was looking forward to our next visit.

She then escorted me back to the waiting area.

"Ms. Bassett, it's been a pleasure and I look forward to seeing you on Friday. Would you please tell Hayes I said hello?"

"Of course I will, Dr. Hanyard."

———

Hayes insisted I come over for dinner, even though I didn't feel like leaving the house again after getting back from my appointment earlier in the day. As usual, dinner was very nice, aside from our conversation about my issues with my daddy. After dinner we went into the family room. I sat down on the couch and watched Hayes as he walked across the room to find a DVD for us to watch. I silently wondered what his faults were. As I listened to him talk confidently about his upcoming trial, I watched how his words smoothly glided past his full lips; how his muscles flexed when he motioned with his hands. Gazing at him, I looked him up and down to take in glimpses of his beautiful, brown skin. I was lost in thought and didn't even realize he was now standing right over me.

"What are you thinking about, beautiful?

"Nothing really…"

"Come on, you were gone. You were thinking about something, share with me."

I looked up into his eyes as he sat on the arm of the couch.

"I was thinking…."

Before I could finish he kissed me on the forehead. "What were you thinking?"

I chuckled. "As I was saying, I was thinking about…"

This time he kissed me on both of my eyelids. "What are you thinking now?"

"About you…"

Hayes' lips were as close to my lips as they could possibly get, without touching. He whispered on my lips. "What about me?"

I wanted to tell him that he made me feel passionate, beautiful, on fire, but I was afraid. William had never made me feel this way, ever. In all the years I dated him I never had this kind of connection with him; the desire for him to touch me, to make love to me, and to be my friend and protector. What I really wanted to do was snatch Hayes off of the arm of the chair and throw myself on top of him. Forget the romance, I thought I might want to investigate and satisfy the primal urge raging inside of me. Instead, I took my hands and grabbed either side of his collar and pulled his lips onto mine. I was a woman; surely I could show him what I was thinking. Soon I was lying underneath him, his hands taking control of my body – strong hands caressing the small of my back; holding my waist; gripping my hips; massaging my shoulders. He slowly lifted his head to look at me. He smiled. His hands glided back to the small of my back.

I returned the smile. "What are you thinking?"

He didn't respond. I could feel his heart beating quickly as his chest heaved up and down.

"I don't want to ruin the moment," he whispered.

"Ruin the moment, with what? You aren't going to give me any bad news, are you?"

Hayes stopped and looked at me. "How much of this is about me and how much of us being together is really about your father?"

I was floored. *Where did that come from?*

"Hayes, you approached me, remember? You asked me out. I may never have said anything to you. It's merely a coincidence that you're considerably older than me and that my parents just happened to get a divorce around the same time we met. I kind of understand why someone else might think something's up with that, but I don't understand why you would? I'm lying here underneath you …and you think this has something to do with my dad? That would be kind of sick, don't you think?"

I put my hands on his chest and softly pushed him off of me as I sat up. I looked away and then down at my hands, as if they held the answer to my questions.

"Vada, I'm…look, I'm just saying, maybe you're

getting something from me that you aren't getting from your dad right now."

"I can't belief this." I spoke barely above a whisper, more to myself than to him.

Hayes sat up and reached out to touch me, but I now had my hands in my lap, and did not respond to his touch.

"Okay, this isn't coming out right. I'm an older man; your dad's an older man. Your relationship with him is strained right now, but our relationship seems to be flourishing. Maybe whatever it is you're not getting from him – paternally, you're getting from me romantically."

"Hmph...I'm speechless. Not sure if this is coming from some clandestine conversation that you had with someone else, who obviously doesn't know me very well, or if you're just trying to play psychiatrist right now."

Bewildered, I stopped speaking long enough to glance around the room, as if searching for the moment right before Hayes mentioned my father. Baffled by the turn of events, I stood and smoothed down my clothes with both hands.

"I think I should leave."

Hayes quickly jumped to his feet to stop me. "I don't want you to leave upset. This is not what I intended to happen. I tried to approach it as delicately as I knew how to. I don't want you to leave, VJ."

I turned to look at him. "I'm not upset, just confused, a little hurt and disappointed, but not upset. Guess you and my dad do have something in common after all." I tightened my lips and raised my brow. "How 'bout that? I suppose it's a good thing I have a psychologist to talk to, huh? Oh, by the way, Dr. Hanyard said to tell you hello." I grabbed my purse and quickly walked out without even looking back.

————

Dee assured me that what happened with me and Hayes was good. I couldn't see it.

"The man wines and dines me, takes me on a fabulous trip, gives me an expensive piece of jewelry, professes his love for me, and then tells me that it's possible that I don't really have similar feelings for him; that I might just be projecting my daddy issues on him?"

Dee was also on her way home from a night out and I could tell she wasn't in the mood I needed her to be in.

"Can you hold off with the drama for a change? Look VJ, it's not as bad as it sounds. Let me tell you what's going on with Hayes right now..."

"How would you know what's going on with him?" The frustration in my voice was with her and Hayes.

"52 or 32, they're all the same. Hayes is really digging you. This thing between y'all is really real. You know what I'm saying? The last few weeks are falling into perspective and he's beginning to realize that he's only known you for a short time and he has already whisked you away to an island, given you a pre-engagement gift, and told you that he's in love with you. The man has basically sealed the deal on marrying you.

He's sprung and he's scared! Scared to death! You are 19 years his junior, you're beautiful, intelligent, and you still have young men sniffing around you. He's questioning what he can really offer you as an older man, when you and I both know that he has just as much, if not more, to offer than any of those other knuckleheads. And honey, if he's half as good at keeping you happy in bed as he is with everything else he does then he wins, hands down."

"What makes you think that's what's going on? How do you know for sure? And why do you always have to take things between men and women to the lowest common denominator?"

"Honestly, I don't know…for sure, but they're all the same. He's just a man. As much as we tease about him being strong, confident, intelligent, and whatever else we say about him, at the end of the day he's just like any other man: overly sensitive and insecure. Now, regarding that lowest common denominator, there's nothing low about it. It's a beautiful thing; it's natural, and it can be the difference between days and nights of utter frustration and a life of bliss. One of these days you'll find out what I'm talking about and, trust me, there's nothing low or dirty about it."

"I hope you're right, about everything. Right now, this whole thing with Hayes is crazy. It just doesn't make sense…to me."

"Like I said, at the end of the day, sweetie, he's still just a man. They're not hard to figure out; they get scared just like we do. They just handle it a little differently. You're young, you're fresh, you make him feel youthful, you give him a different outlook on things, and, most importantly, you make him happy. Give him a day or two and he'll call you. And if, for some reason, he doesn't, you call him. Y'all simply need to talk this through. I promise you, y'all are going to live happily ever after."

"What makes you think you know so much?"

"First of all, I've never seen you happier…and I've known you for a long time. I know how I felt the first time a younger cat asked me out. It's no different for a man, an ego is an ego, is an ego. And anyway, I want to believe that your story is going to have a happy ending."

"Happy endings are only in fairy tales, Dee. This is real life."

"Let me dream, okay? Look, I have another call coming in. I think it's this guy I met a little earlier tonight. I'll call you back."

———

June 18, 2012

Hayes actually thinks I'm attracted to him because of the problems that I'm having with my dad. Dee laughed at me when I told her what happened. She thinks she has all the answers, but nothing she said made me feel any better. I don't understand why he feels the way he does. Makes me think he really just gets off wining and dining me. I haven't known him long, but from the very beginning I thought he was grounded and honest…the kind of man that any woman would want to marry and have a family with. If I'm honest with myself, he does sort of remind me of my dad. My dad has, had, some admirable qualities: he was a great father, a great provider. In light of everything that has transpired over the last few months, probably just an adequate husband; he was a super communicator, a great teacher; a wonderful life coach; he was compassionate, attentive, fun… I suppose he's still all of those things. Maybe my father, as I knew him, was a lie. So, how do I deal with both of them now, my dad and Hayes?

Okay, that wasn't the line of thought I was initially going for. So what if Hayes has some of the same qualities as my dad. So what! So what…? Why is he tripping?

I have to remember to ask Dee where she was earlier tonight and who this guy is that she met?

THANKFUL FOR: seeing the words in black and white. Sometimes hearing them is too much

Chapter 15

June 19, 2012

Hayes didn't call me this morning. Oh, well… I planned on working from home today anyway. Guess I'll stick to my plans. I have plenty to do and I can always have my secretary transfer calls to me at home. She can fax any documents that can't be emailed. I sure wish I was going to see Dr. Hanyard today. Just saw her yesterday, but I sure wish I could talk with her today. I don't want to lose Hayes over this "stuff" with my dad. Hope he calls…

THANKFUL FOR: hope…

———

After calling Carolyn, I pushed a few papers around on my desk for about 30 or 40 minutes before picking up the phone again to make another call.

"Good morning, Mom, what're you doing?"

"Good morning, Vada. Why are you calling me from home? Is everything okay?"

"I'm working from home this week."

"This week, are you sick?"

"No, I'm not sick. I just don't feel like going into the office this week."

"Is this about your father? If it is, don't do this. Don't let whatever is going on with him keep you away from work, Vada. This is getting a little out of hand now.

"It seems like everybody is somehow under the impression that I should be emotionally detached from everything that has happened between you and Daddy."

"I don't think anybody is saying that. I'm certainly not. I'm just saying, I don't want you to be so consumed by the divorce that it begins to have an impact on the rest of your life. You have such a wonderful support system: you have me to talk with; Dee loves you more than a blood sister could ever love you, maybe even more than she loves her own siblings; and I'm sure Hayes is being very supportive."

I didn't want to hear any more of what was being said. "Mother..."

"What is it Vada? Honey, don't let this take control of you."

"Really, I'm not. I mean, I started seeing a psychologist yesterday day."

"That's wonderful, sweetie. Take control of the situation and work it to your benefit. Your dad still loves you just as much as he always has. If you have to think about a relationship, spend more time thinking about the one you're building with Hayes and less about what has happened between me and your dad."

"From what Hayes said to me last night, they're one in the same."

"What does that mean?"

"Hayes seems to think that I might be dating him because, let's see, he said something to the effect of, maybe whatever I'm not getting from Daddy, paternally, I might be getting from him romantically. Isn't that just crazy?"

For a brief moment there was silence. I could almost hear my mother thinking.

"Mom, are you still there? Did you hear what I said?"

"I did…it's kind of ironic that Hayes would say that."

"Why would you say that?"

"Cecilia and I were just talking about that the other day."

Unintentionally, I snapped at my mother. "What? You too, you think I'm dating him because of Daddy? So now I'm only limited to dating guys who fulfill my need for a daddy? Is everybody crazy?"

"No, sweetheart, calm down. I don't think anybody is saying that. It's just that you're pretty distraught about your dad, and Hayes is…Hayes is a bit older and he does dote on you just like your dad always did. Don't you see the irony in that?"

"I suppose I would if I had initiated the relationship, but Hayes approached me. He asked me out…"

"And maybe you accepted because…"

"Because he's older? That's ridiculous. If you want to know the truth, Dee and I had been checking him out a long time before he ever spoke to me. For about a year he walked by my office, no less than three times a day, and he would always look in and smile. I suspect he walked by more than that, but I was either away from my desk or otherwise occupied, so I may not have seen him. An even more relevant point is that I was dating William or else, with Dee's coaxing, I probably would have said something to Hayes long before now. I don't know. I can assure you, though I may seem to be a bit over the top about Daddy, my relationship with Hayes is based on its own merits. I really like him. I really do. He's a refreshing change from William. Okay, so he's a bit older; I have no control over that. I would be a liar if I said I didn't find that the slightest bit attractive…and at the end of the day, if some of the qualities I find attractive about him are similar to Daddy's…so what? Daddy taught me what I should expect from a man. I love my daddy, and I can see myself being in love with a man like Hayes."

"Well, then, you should have your butt at work!" My mother laughed. "You've certainly confirmed that some things will never change. Even when you were a little girl you were dramatic."

"I was never dramatic, Mother."

"Oh, really; do you remember the time your dad had an emergency deposition out of town and you didn't find out about it until you got home from school? You actually cried yourself sick until he called that night. As soon as you talked with him you were miraculously healed of all suffering? Do you remember that?"

"So, what's your point?" I smiled as I recalled the incident.

"Drama queen…"

"Uhh, sometimes you can be so, so..."

"So, what, mindful? Well, what you need to do now is talk with Hayes, and then talk with your dad. Get your house back in order, Vada Jade."

"Yes, ma'am, I certainly will. First call to order, what

are you doing this evening?"

"Why, what do you have in mind?"

"Come over; let me cook dinner for you."

"You sure you don't want to invite Hayes over?"

"No, I think I'll call him and find out what he's doing for lunch. I know he's preparing for a trial next week, but he has to stop to eat…I hope. You know what?"

"What, sweetheart?"

"I think I'll send him a gift basket to apologize for walking out on him last night."

"Girl, you walked out on 'THAT' last night? You are surely no daughter of mine." Her laughter was hearty, unrestrained, and contagious. "Wait until I tell Cecilia!"

I found myself laughing just as hard. It was good to hear her laugh like that.

———

The talk with my mom did me some good. After getting off the phone, I immediately called "Say It with Wine Gift Baskets" and had a wonderful cabernet sauvignon gift basket sent to Hayes, along with a card apologizing for acting like a child and walking out on him. I wanted to see him, and I promised myself I wouldn't react so rashly in the future. I also wanted to ask him to be patient with me because it wouldn't be long before I was back to my old self. I was convinced of that.

I had requested the basket be delivered before noon. Obviously, they did as I asked because Hayes must have called me as soon as he received it.

"Hello."

"VJ, nobody has ever sent me a gift basket before. I wish I had thought of it first. Thank you."

"Hayes, you weren't out of line last night, I was. I guess I'm a little more sensitive than I thought. I know that you care about me. I shouldn't have stormed out without talking to you. If you haven't eaten yet, will you allow me to take you out for to lunch to make it up to you? I'd like to see you and I don't want to wait until tonight."

"I don't want to wait either…"

"How about, I come and pick you up?"

"You don't have to do that; I can meet you somewhere."

"No, I want to come pick you up. I can be there in 45 minutes, if that's not too late."

"I'll be ready when you get here."

———

After a two-hour lunch, Hayes and I went back to the office. He wanted to wrap up some things and I wanted to talk with my secretary to find out if there was anything pressing that needed to be addressed. I made a quick call to Dee, to gloat over the fact that Hayes and I had made up. Afterwards, before leaving, I went to the copier room to make some copies.

As I approached the room I could hear two women chirping away. Initially, I couldn't make out who they were, but I was able to clearly make out what they were talking about – me and Hayes.

Beverly was speaking confidently, like she personally knew Hayes. "Look, I don't know what kind of game Vada Bassett is trying to play, but she's not even his type. There is no doubt in my mind that the whole thing is about sex. He's old enough to be her father; it can't be anything else. She's his little play thing."

Trepidation gripped Iris' face as she nervously looked from side to side. "I don't know. She's real nice and super intelligent. She's never struck me as someone that would put herself out like that. I heard there were a couple of other attorneys that had asked her out and she just stopped them cold in their tracks, but that was some time ago."

"That may be the case, but Hayes is a partner with the firm. I can assure you, when she asked him out, and she had to have asked him, he jumped at the opportunity. That man's wife died a few years ago and women have been shamelessly throwing themselves at him ever since. She's no different. Why wouldn't he play before he gets married again? Get all of that out of his system? I've been out with him a couple of times, so I know what I'm talking about. Age wise, he and I have much more in common than they do. I just don't know if I'm ready for a serious relationship."

"I guess. That joker is a 'faune' one, though. The woman that gets him will have hit the jackpot because he really is a nice guy. You've been divorced, what, two years now? Why haven't you been a little more aggressive about getting to know him?"

"I don't want to be thrown into the same category as

those other women chasing behind him. It has to be done in a way that he thinks it was his idea."

"I know that's right!" Iris clapped her hands, and they both broke out into cackling laughter.

I took that as my cue to enter the room. My initial thought was to correct everything that I had just heard, but then I reasoned, why? Obviously, they don't know me or Hayes. I came to the conclusion that my presence alone would be enough to shock them out of their expensive pumps.

"Good afternoon, I knew I heard someone in here talking. Beverly and…" I pointed at the other woman. "…Iris?"

Even before they responded, their faces spoke volumes. It was priceless.

Beverly, the more outspoken of the two, spoke first. "Oh, uhm, Vada, hi, it's good to see you. It seems like I haven't seen you around the office in a while. It's good to see you."

"Yes, it seems like it has been a while."

Iris chimed in. "You look great! Life has been good to you, no?"

I shrugged my shoulders. "I don't have any complaints."

As I spoke, I placed my document on the copier with my left hand. The fluorescent lights reflected off of my bracelet just right, creating a blinding kaleidoscope of colors throughout the room.

Iris was in awe. "That's a beautiful bracelet, Vada."

"Oh, you mean this? Thank you. It was a gift."

Visibly perturbed, Beverly had difficulty hiding her contempt. "It's what, a couple of carats?"

"I don't know; it may be six or seven. I'm not sure."

Iris smiled. "It's beautiful. I almost thought it was an engagement ring."

"Yeah, well, you never know…"

Beverly and Iris turned and looked at each other.

"Well, ladies, let me make these copies so I can get out of here and get ready for my dinner date tonight. It was nice seeing both of you." I turned my attention to the copier as they walked out of the room.

Smiling to myself, I was satisfied that I'd given them more than enough to talk about now.

————

June 22, 2012

The week ended uneventfully. Hayes and I made up and we have a date to go salsa dancing tomorrow. Next weekend we're going to go stepping again. He thinks he can out dance me. We'll see. This all started up again because we danced in his den the other night. Don't get me wrong, he's a great dancer, but he's never salsa danced before, and I'm the salsa queen.

I told him about the conversation in the copier room. He laughed! He thought it was hilarious. He said a couple of the older guys had asked him about me and had given him the old "pat on the back." He thought that was funny too.

I met with Dr. Hanyard today. Of course, it was great. I like that lady. I really like that lady! I told her what happened with me and Hayes the evening after I had my first appointment with her. I also returned prepared to talk about the "fabric of my life." Made me really think about how everything that happened during the week was related. I was kind of proud of how I handled the situation with Beverly and Iris. Gave me a little satisfaction to not only show them up but also shut them up, at the same time. To let them see that this thing between me and Hayes is real.

THANKFUL FOR: having the real thing...and for Dr. Hanyard

Chapter 16

June 25, 2012

Great weekend! Hopefully this will be another great week. I'll certainly try to do better by everyone. Hayes is in trial all week. I'll be busy at work. I have my appointment with Dr. Hanyard tomorrow. Probably won't see Hayes until Saturday. No matter what happens with the trial, he'll have dinner with his team Friday night, probably every night until they finish the trial.

It was a great weekend, even with seeing William…and his wife. Yeah, HIS WIFE! As we were leaving the club Hayes and I ran into them in the parking deck. Apparently they had just had dinner. There's so much I could say, but why? Afterward, Hayes told me he recognized William. Aside from being a little ashamed for being too stupid to know I was dating a married guy, it was pretty anti-climatic. Hayes assured me it wasn't me. That there were some men who took great pride in trying to have it all…a wife, a family, and an active dating life. We were both glad I had moved on to something better. When Hayes dropped me off I was still exhausted from all of the dancing we did, so I didn't bother calling Dee.

Guess I better stop here and get ready for work.

THANFUL FOR: salsa dancing with a good man

———

"VJ."

"Yes, Carolyn."

"I have a call for you. It's Mr. Townes. Do you want to take the call or should I take a message?"

"Put him through, I'll take it."

I knew I would be getting a call from him, after he saw me with Hayes…and after introducing me to his wife.

"Good morning, William. What's up? Oh, let me answer that for you. Perhaps you're calling because I met your wife last night?"

"Come on V, don't be like that?"

"Be like what? You're lucky I even took the call. Really, what do you want?"

"I had to call you to tell you how good you looked last night. Life must really be treating you well."

"You called me to tell me that I looked good last night? Did you and your 'wife' have a long discussion about how good I looked?"

"V, I don't even know why you're going there. Don't let me get started on that sugar daddy you were with."

"Don't make me regret taking this call. Let me rephrase that, don't make me further regret taking this call. If that's all you called to say then this conversation is over."

"No, no, no…for real, I called you this morning to tell you that after seeing you last night, I realized how much I miss our friendship. You know, you were always the better part of my day…always. I wish we could, you

185

know, maybe, have lunch or dinner sometimes. I would love to talk with you about how much I've changed; how much spending time with you taught me about myself, especially towards the end. I think I'm more responsible now, that I consider other people's feelings and not just my own. Deg, V, you taught me that life was really bigger than me. I looked at you and couldn't believe that I had been exposed to someone as beautiful as you, and I blew it."

I chuckled. "Are you serious? Okay, first of all, we obviously were never really friends. Friends don't treat each other the way you treated me; friends don't lie or mislead each other either. Well, at least not anyone that I have ever considered a real friend. That woman you were with last night, you didn't just marry her. You were either dating her when we were dating, and I cringe when I think about this, or you were married to her while we were together. Either way, you have no idea how to be 'my' friend. And the fact that you have the audacity to refer to our relationship as though it were some platonic high school frivolity baffles me. You asked me to marry you – more than once…more than once. You're pathetic! Obviously, from the moment you met me until last night, everything about you, about us, about our relationship was a lie. So, don't call me playing games. Your charm doesn't work on me anymore. I see you for what you really are, for what you always were…and that's it. Now, I wish you and your wife a happy life together."

Nothing about William had changed. He was still the

very same arrogant, self-absorbed, William. I merely saw him through different eyes now.

"V, some of what happened was just as much your fault as it was mine. You have to admit that; right? You didn't want me to tell you everything about my life." His words were sharp and condescending. "You weren't overly concerned that you never came to my house. I mean, come on, you knew that there might have been a possibility that I was seeing someone else, but you never asked, never seemed bothered. You're a big girl. You could have done your homework."

"So, you're saying it's my fault that you are a liar and philanderer?"

"We never made love, V, so you can't call me a philanderer."

"Oh, but you're not denying you're a liar? Who does that? I mean, really, who lies to that extent, other than a sociopath? So, you're saying, it was okay to lie to me and screw around on me because we didn't have sex?"

"Look, V, I loved you, girl. I respected your wishes. You wanted to wait until you got married, and that's what I did. You're an intelligent woman; you had to know I was having sex with somebody."

"Okay...so the fact that we never had sex; the fact that you respected my wishes; and the fact that I'm intelligent and I should have known better, excuses the truth – that you were not only freakin' women all over town, but that you were doing it with women other than the woman you're clearly married to. Oh, yeah, I forgot, again, while you were dating me. Oh, yeah, yeah, and how could I forget this? And you tried to get with my girl Dee. Now that my eyes are wide open, I don't even know what I saw in you, other than the fact that you didn't pressure me, one way or the other. That was my fault. I was comfortable. Psss…but you know what? This conversation is a waste of my time. The best thing you could have ever done for me was to walk out my house that day. So, thank you. Now do me a favor and lose my number."

I hung up the phone and felt vindicated in leaving that part of my life behind. I also felt okay with taking responsibility for my part in the relationship – being lazy, complacent, and comfortable for all the wrong reasons, and taking William at face value, when, clearly, Dee was right about him all along.

Chapter 17

Today, I was looking just as forward to my visit with Dr. Hanyard as I was the second time I came to see her. My visits with the doctor have been very relaxing, yet extremely eye opening. Today would probably be no different. As I sat in the waiting room I thought about my schedule. I also thought about my last conversation with William; he hadn't changed at all, not that I had expected him to. *But it's not unreasonable for a person to expect another person to grow or progress in some way over time; is it?* While I was in the middle of my thought, Dr. Hanyard entered the waiting room.

"Good morning, VJ."

"Good morning, Dr. Hanyard. It's good to see you this morning."

The doctor ushered me into her office and pointed at my favorite seat. "Come on back and let's get this show on the road. How are you today?"

"I'm doing well."

"That's good to hear. What's been going on with you?"

"You know, maybe I'm still making too much out of everything – my mom and dad, Hayes, my ex. I don't know how to make all of the thoughts slow down or, better yet, go away. Well, first of all, in addition to calling me yesterday, William, my ex, called my mother too, just to say hello. He happened to mention to her that he was involved in some philanthropic endeavor. When my mother told me about it I wasn't impressed. I actually wanted to spit, but instead I was nice. I told her it was okay if she didn't tell me when he called her. I don't know that she completely appreciates that he's not on my list of 'all-time favorite people.'"

"So, you don't want your ex-boyfriend calling your mother?"

"No, I don't care if he calls my mother; I don't have any control over that. I just don't want to hear about it. Is that bad?"

"I don't know, is it? What would make it bad?"

I looked at the doctor, expecting a little more direction, even though I knew there wasn't going to be any. I knew her prevailing method involved making me draw my own conclusions.

"Dr. Hanyard, you're so sneaky. I don't really know if it's bad or not; I just know that I don't want to talk to my ex, talk about my ex, and I certainly don't want to hear about all of his 'so called' good deeds, particularly after all of the dirt he did to me. You know what, he's not my problem. Can we talk about something else, please?"

Dr. Hanyard nodded her head in agreement.

"Okay, what initially brought me to you was my parents' divorce. As their marriage was falling apart, I was so self-absorbed that I overlooked what was actually going on right in front of me. So, most recently I've been doing this, uhm, self – what do you call it – self-evaluation, to determine whether or not I'm self-absorbed to the extent that I'm not paying keen attention to what's going on around me."

Dr. Hanyard tilted her head to one side. "Is it, perhaps, possible that your parents purposely hid their problems from you to protect you from what was going on? And while you're thinking about that, have you always internalized things?"

I didn't have to think long or hard to answer either question. "Well, yeah, I suppose as an only child, because I didn't have anybody there to bounce things off of, I just kind of sorted things out on my own."

"What about friends, did you have close friends growing up?"

"I did, but I think I was their 'go to girl,' so I didn't necessarily confide in them because... I just didn't."

"If I can go back just a bit, you never really commented on whether or not it was possible that your parents kept their problems hidden from you. I apologize; that was my fault. I shouldn't have asked two questions at the same time."

"No, that's okay. I don't think they really hid anything from me. It was just that I was in school then I moved out, so I just wasn't there to see what was going on."

"Do you think your being there would have made a difference?"

"Absolutely not," I smiled. "I'm not that jaded."

"Okay, I'm just asking." Dr. Hanyard smiled as she scribbled on her pad. "Tell me, VJ, if you had to describe your complete childhood in two words, what would those two words be?"

I searched my mind for the appropriate expressions. "Two words, let's see, two words…I would have to say comfortable and harmonious."

The doctor stretched her mouth a bit and simultaneously wrote copious notes on her pad. "Really, comfortable and harmonious, that's interesting." She smiled and nodded her head, with what resembled parental approval. "Tell me a little bit more about that."

"Well, my childhood was extremely comfortable. I grew up with both of my parents present. I had great friends. I had all of my grandparents, lots of cousins, and lots of great experiences. I can't think of one moment in my life when I didn't feel loved. I've always told people that I led a charmed life. My mom and dad also had me involved in all kinds of activities that kept me occupied and busy. So, to me, my life was in complete harmony."

"And now…?"

"Oh, I see what you're doing, Dr. Hanyard. Okay, the truth is, I still have all of that, of course, with the exception of my grandparents. And, in addition, I now have a great career, a beautiful home, a great best friend, a good life, and Hayes…"

"So, would you say your life is any less comfortable or harmonious now?"

I stopped short of rolling my eyes at her. "On the surface, no, it isn't."

"On the surface, okay, so what's preventing it from being either comfortable or harmonious?"

"Oh, this is so unfair." I knew I was being made to acknowledge the fact that things weren't as bad as I was making them out to be. "My life is, actually, quite comfortable. It is, though, a little out of harmony, just a little because…" My voice trailed off.

"I'm sorry, I can't hear you."

"I said, because of my parents' divorce I began to question my father's love for me."

"You began to question it; do you still question it?"

"I know my father loves me."

"Of course you do and of course he does, VJ. So, over the last few visits we've determined that there are a lot of things going on: shift in family dynamics, a loss and a grieving, but ultimately the issue is love; right? So, the shift in family dynamics can be disorienting to even the most stable individuals. We know that; right? Of course, that shift often involves loss, sometimes gain – new baby, new spouse, new step-parent – but when it involves loss, the grief that follows can be thought of as a form of development. Unfortunately, all love stories, if you will, come to an end, even those that last a lifetime – a spouse dies, children grow up and leave the nest, and siblings grow up and grow in different directions, spouses divorce; should I continue?

In a family there are lots of different facets of love or love stories. So, when a loss like that hits us, it hits us hard. It can be difficult to know what to do with it, or even how to bear it, in some instances. There is a mourning period, like there is with death, which is the ultimate loss. Yet, in this instance, mourning, in some respect, is a process whereby we can learn to accept, not necessarily the end of love, but a change in the dynamics of love. Towards the end of that process we start feeling whole again, if we allow ourselves to. What's interesting is the self you get back may not necessarily be the same as the self you relinquished to your relationship, whether it involves spouses, a parent and a child, or two siblings. That's just a fancy way to say wounds heal, but they sometimes leave scars.

When you take the opportunity to work through the loss, therapeutically, then you find that there's more to gain than just surviving the breakup or the change, if you will. There's also the possibility of becoming more than you were previously. You hopefully develop the ability to undertake or withstand the next experience of love in its moments of sadness, as well as joy, because there will always be both – moments of sadness and moments of joy. That's life, right?"

I considered what I thought Dr. Hanyard was trying to say: This whole thing I was dealing with was not a loss of love, but a change in my relationship with my father, that didn't involve my father loving me any less. Really, when the emotion was put aside, the change was superficial because he was still my dad and I was still his daughter; and our relationship would always have moments of sadness and moments of joy, and that there was the possibility to grow from each pivotal moment we shared. Well, that's what I got from it, anyway.

Chapter 18

June 29, 2012

Hayes called me before I left the office and told me his family would be in town tomorrow. Family meaning: both of his brothers and their wives and both of his parents. Apparently, they're all coming for the fourth of July, but somehow they all decided to spend the week with him. So he is taking next week off to entertain them. Of course, my mother and I are invited over for dinner tomorrow night and on the fourth. This is going to be interesting. I'm excited, but nervous about meeting the rest of his family. Well, Leah (and my mom) will be there, so I should be okay. I haven't extended the invitation to my mother yet, but I'm sure she's going to want to go. While I'm at Hayes' house tomorrow I'll ask him if it's okay to invite Dee and her family over for his barbecue on the fourth. There's always safety in numbers.

THANKFUL FOR: the next step, meeting the family...

———

The drive to Hayes' house was quite interesting. Mom was in psychiatrist mode. She knew I could handle myself with his family, but she was concerned about how his parents would receive me. It's not like that hadn't already crossed my mind.

"So, honey, you should be relaxed but in attorney

mode with Hayes' parents; don't you think?"

"Mother, really? I don't think so. I want to be relaxed and natural. I'm just going to be myself, so stop making me more nervous than I am already." I reached over and hit her on the leg to reprimand her.

Playfully, my mother pushed my hand away. "You better keep both of your hands on the steering wheel. Can I ask you something?"

"If I say no you're going to ask me anyway, right?"

"Yes, that's correct." My mother laughed. "How many times did you change clothes before you left the house?"

"How do you...three times before I decided to wear what I have on. What made you ask me that? Is something wrong with what I have on?" I'm sure I looked panic stricken.

"No, not at all, I recall when I met your grandparents. Your father didn't even tell me we were going to see them. It's been a long time, but I vaguely remember having on something sexy for him, so I was mortified when I realized he was taking me to meet them. He assured me I looked fine, but just imagine, 41 years ago, what your grandparents must have been thinking." Mom shook her head as she laughed.

"So what are you trying to say, do I look sexy?"

Laughing even harder now, my mother could barely catch her breath. "No, no, you look fine. I was just thinking: Had I had the opportunity to pick out something appropriate for meeting your father's parents, I would have torn my closet apart looking for the right thing to wear. And I know you, daughter. Things have to be just so."

"Mother, are you purposely trying to make me more nervous? But really, I look okay, right?"

"You look beautiful. Know what, though? I can't imagine Hayes has told his parents anything about you, except for the fact that he's seeing someone. He's a very grown man with grown children, and little grandchildren, as well as a successful attorney, so I'm sure he doesn't find it necessary to get his parents' approval about who to date, but you have to know they're going to be surprised by…your, let's say, youth. That aside, I think the more important issue is going to be how much he cares about you. Well, I guess, when you look at both things together, your age and the fact that he thinks he's in love with you, they might be a little indifferent. Honestly, I don't know, though. I really don't."

I chose not to reply. I didn't know what to say. Just when I thought the issue with our ages was fading away, here it was rearing its ugly head again. I was so wrapped up in my parents that I didn't even think about what it was going to be like to meet Hayes' parents. As I pulled into the driveway my mom popped her seatbelt and turned to look at me.

"You okay? You ready?"

I shrugged my shoulders. "I guess. I'm just going to be myself. What else is there for me to do? You have single-handedly managed to tell me my future in-laws are going to hate me because I'm too young for my boyfriend and that what I have on is ugly. I'm as ready as I'm going to get." I turned and stared at her. "So let's go meet my perspective in-laws."

My mother took her index finger and poked me in the shoulder. "What did I tell you? Just always so dramatic..."

We laughed as we got out of the car.

I escorted her to the front door. It appears Leah saw my car when we pulled up, so she opened the door just as I prepared to ring the doorbell. She greeted us holding Owen. Surprisingly, she reached out and gave me a hug, which really caught me off guard.

"Hi, Leah, this is my mom, Lois Bassett. Mom, this is Hayes' daughter, Leah."

It must have been a real love fest going on in the house because Leah reached out and hugged my mom, too. Mom was used to being hugged by her clients, so she wasn't quite as surprised as I was with Leah's show of affection. Leah then closed the door behind us.

"Come on, everybody's sitting out on the patio. I'm sorry, where are my manners? Can I offer you ladies something to drink before we go outside?"

My mom and I turned and looked at each other then I turned and looked back at Leah. "No, I think we're fine right now."

Shaking Owen on her hip, Leah turned and looked at my mom. "You, Mrs. Bassett, would you like something to drink?"

Shaking her head, my mother smiled at Leah and played with the baby. "No, I think I'm fine for now. But thank you."

Leah walked us through the kitchen to the patio. "Oh, VJ, cute outfit by the way."

"Thanks, Leah." I turned and looked at my mom and stuck my tongue out at her.

When Hayes saw us he jumped up and quickly walked over to the patio door. He greeted me and mom with a kiss on our cheeks. His very handsome, stately looking father stood up, as any gentleman would do when ladies enter the room.

He extended his hand to shake my mom's hand. "You must be the lovely lady that Hayes is so excited about us meeting. It is a pleasure to make your acquaintance. And this must be your lovely daughter." He looked at me as he held my mother's hand.

Mom smiled. "Well, I'm Lois Bassett, the lovely lady's mother."

I promise you, if it had been possible, it felt like time stopped. Mr. Vishmell stood there looking at me, as he held my mother's hand. Hayes quickly stepped in and put his arm around my shoulder.

"Mom, Dad, this is Vada Jade Bassett and her mother Dr. Lois Bassett."

Every single, silver hair on Hayes' mother bob remained in place as she turned her head to look at us. Though her eyes betrayed her, she smiled. "It is a pleasure meeting both of you. Please come and have a seat."

As Hayes directed us to our seats, he introduced us to the other couple silently observing the show. "VJ, Lois, this is my brother, Harris, and his wife, Dana. Harris, Dana…" Hayes touched the small of my back. "…VJ Bassett and her mother Dr. Lois Bassett."

Harris stood to shake our hands. "It's a pleasure ladies; looking forward to a fun evening."

His smile offered hope that the night would go smoother, after that fiasco of an introduction with his father.

Dana didn't stand, but she nodded her head, smiled, and offered her hand. "It's nice that both of you could make it."

After we sat down, it felt like several seconds passed before anyone said anything. So, mom broke the proverbial ice.

"So what is everyone drinking?"

Dana sipped from her glass before speaking. "Mmm…Helen makes great basil lemonade…with vodka. You should try it." She looked over at her mother-in-law and held up her glass.

Laughing, Mom looked at me. "VJ, I'm not sure about you, but I think I'd like to have a glass of lemonade."

Everyone laughed just as Hayes' other brother and his other sister-in-law walked up. They were dressed like they had been working out.

Apparently, his sister-in-law was an extrovert. "Hey, what's so funny? I imagine one of these ladies is Hayes' friend that he can't stop talking about?"

Once again silence, as all eyes turned towards me and mom.

Leah, who was still standing in the open patio door with Owen in her arms, saw that I was uncomfortable. "You know what? I'll get a fresh pitcher of lemonade and a few more glasses. VJ, would you come help me, please?"

Great, Leah is now my new best friend. She saved me from the lions' pit. I'm sure things will only get better as the night goes on.

Chapter 19

Dinner was fun and everyone was pleasant. After meeting Tyler, Hayes' other brother, and Collie, which is short for Colleen, Hayes' second sister-in-law, any tension that may have been present subsided. It didn't hurt that Mrs. Vishmell kept the basil lemonade flowing the entire evening. I offered to help Hayes with dinner, but it seemed like his mother was always in there with him, so I played guest the entire night. Of course, there was no PDA, at all. On a few occasions, I found myself getting a little nervous when Hayes sat too close to me. I'm sure he was baffled that I seemed so standoffish, but I felt like I was under the microscope and I didn't want to be seen as the young plaything. In spite of the under stated tension, I always knew when he was looking at me. I could feel it. I would steal a look at him and smile. I felt like we were in high school. He might be 52 years old, but we both shared a childlike respect for his parents. Well, for his mother.

I caught Mrs. Vishmell looking at me, too. I didn't get the impression that she disliked me, but she was doing the best she could to contain her disapproval. I could tell, and I'm sure everyone else could, as well. I will be the first to say, in addition to not finding an opportunity to be alone with Hayes; I made sure I didn't mistakenly find myself alone with Mrs. Vishmell either. I didn't want to have to deal with that tonight. I wanted to get familiar with his family, and for them to get familiar with me. That would be enough for one night. At 8:30 p.m. my mother cornered me on my way to the bathroom and suggested we leave. I was actually thinking the same thing. Mr. and Mrs. Vishmell looked tired and I didn't want to wear out my welcome with them on the first night.

When I went back out on the patio, where everyone had gathered after dinner, I sat next to Hayes on a wicker settee.

"I think mom and I are going to leave. I hope you don't mind," I whispered.

His mother and father were playing a really serious game of bid whist against Harris and Dana, while my mother talked with Tyler and Collie. Leah and Solomon had already left to put their kids to bed.

Hayes looked disappointed, but he knew just as well as I did that it was time to end the night, at least for me and mom. He took this as an opportunity for us to sneak away for a few minutes. Grabbing me by the hand, Hayes led me through the kitchen into the dining room. Once we were in the dining room he put his arms around me and gave me a long, soft kiss.

"I've wanted to do that all evening."

I smiled and inhaled his scent.

"Thank you for coming to meet my family. And look, I know you think there's something going on with my mother, and there is, but it's not you personally. Celine was her daughter-in-law for a long time, so it'll just take her a little while to get adjusted to me being with another woman. If you felt uncomfortable at all tonight I apologize. If you want me to, I can talk to her."

That was the last thing I wanted. "No, everything's fine. I understand how your mom feels. I'm sure she didn't expect you to be alone forever, but I'm also sure she expected someone a little older. Hence, your dad's little faux pas earlier this evening. I'm sure everything will be fine."

I placed my hands on either side of his face and kissed him again. "Look, let's get out of here. I don't want you mother to think I'm seducing you."

Hayes laughed. "I wish you were."

As I turned to walk away, he grabbed me by my waist and pulled me up against his body and began kissing me on the back of my neck.

I reached back and palmed his head. "Uh, uh…Hayes…"

He stopped and wrapped his arms around me. "I want you, VJ – more tonight than I've ever wanted you."

"I know, babe. Let's go back out on the patio, so I can get my mom and say good night."

Hayes followed me to the patio. It didn't appear that anyone had missed us, so I grabbed my mom by the hand to help her out of her seat.

"I'd like to thank everyone for a lovely evening. It was really nice meeting all of you, and Mrs. Vishmell your lemonade is the best I've ever had. I look forward to seeing everyone on the fourth."

Mom also bid her farewells before Hayes walked us out to the car.

Before we could get out of the driveway my mom

started in on me. "Where were you and Hayes? His mother didn't say anything, but she turned to look at the kitchen about 50 times." Mom laughed. "Were you getting a quickie?"

"Mother! What is wrong with you? You know what? You had way too many of those lemonades. Seriously, though, how do you think tonight went?"

Mother sighed. "Well, it was nice."

"Mom, no, really, do I have to just come out and ask you what you think Mrs. Vishmell thought about me? You're just going to make me ask you, huh?"

"You know what? I can understand Hayes being oblivious to his mother's feelings because he's a 52 year old man, but you have to know that woman loved his wife and is going to have a very difficult time accepting you, a woman young enough to be his daughter, as his wife, not that accepting any other woman wouldn't be difficult, but, VJ, you and Leah are practically the same age."

If I turned to look at my mother now, I knew I would get emotional, so I detached myself from the situation, much like I did when I was in court.

"So, what about everyone else; what do you think they thought about me…and Hayes?

"Leah and Solomon, check; Harris and Dana, check; Tyler and Collie, check plus. Collie is nine years younger than her husband, so they're all for you and Hayes, and Richard Thomas Vishmell is a man. I bet as soon as he gets Hayes alone, he's going to give his son an 'attaboy.'"

Mom broke out in hysterical laughter.

As she was laughing my cell phone rang. It was Dee.

"Hey, who is that laughing like that?"

"It's Mom. She just told a joke that's only funny to her."

"Tell Mama Bassett I said hello."

I looked over at my mother, who was wiping tears from her eyes. "Mom, Dee said hello."

"Tell her I said hi. Oh, on the fourth of July Helen is going to be glad Hayes is with you, after she meets Dee."

As I stopped at the red light I glanced over at my mother.

"What is Mom saying, VJ?"

"Girl, you don't want to know."

"So, how did it go tonight? What happened?"

"Let's just say, my work is cut out for me with Hayes' mother."

"Well, VJ, I mean, you and Hayes make a beautiful couple, but his parents are in their 80's and I can't imagine that at least one of them wouldn't have a problem with you. If it wasn't your age it would be something else, but you knew that."

"Yeah, you're right. I just never stopped to think about it before now."

My mom quickly opened her car door after I pulled into her driveway. "Are you coming in, sweetie?"

"No, I think I'm just going to go on home. I don't know about you, but it was a long evening for me."

Mom leaned over and kissed me on the cheek. "All

jokes aside, the evening was actually fine. I don't think you have anything to worry about. I stand behind what I said earlier in the evening, though. Hayes is a grown man and I don't think his mother or father, or anyone else, for that matter, has any influence over who he chooses to date or marry. But honey, just remember one thing: big, pink elephant. Call me later on if you need to talk."

"Okay."

I could hear Dee on the other end of the phone. "What did Mama Bassett say about elephants?"

Mom was right. I was the big, pink elephant standing in the middle of the room.

————

June 30, 2012

How did I overlook the fact that Hayes' (older) parents would have a problem with his relationship with me? I've been too preoccupied with the divorce. Under normal circumstances, I would never have let details like that slip by. And that's a pretty big detail. I was prepared to be scrutinized by his children, but not his parents. Mrs. Vishmell was clearly disappointed. Not so much with me as a person, just my age. It was also clear she could have handled Hayes' new relationship better had it been with my mother. And the big, pink elephant comment my mom made, she's right. Either Hayes completely overlooked the age issue with his parents or he just didn't care. Well, I'm not going to do anything extra to win their...her approval. I'm going to be myself and hope Mrs. Vishmell eventually realizes my relationship with Hayes isn't fly-by-night.

THANKFUL FOR: July 4th, second chances

Chapter 20

July 6, 2012

By the time the fourth of July rolled around Mrs. Vishmell had nothing but love for me. She also got along really well with Dee, who didn't understand what my problem was. Dee thought Mrs. Vishmell was real cool. It was the basil lemonade. Quincy had a great time with Lydia, and Dee's dad also had a great time. Hayes pulled out all the stops. And, most importantly, we acted like a couple the entire day. I'm pretty certain everyone in the Vishmell family ganged up on Mrs. Vishmell. They must have had a big, old, family pow-wow. Well, whatever or whoever it was, I appreciate it. I'm sure Hayes does too. Hayes' family invited me and mom over for their last Friday in town. We went out for dinner, but came back to Hayes' house for cocktails. The night ended with a sure seal of approval from everyone in the Vishmell family – Mom and I were even included in a family photo.

THANKFUL FOR: Love + Understanding = Acceptance

───

On Sunday, Hayes came over to my house for some alone time. It felt good to have him all to myself, after an entire week of sharing him with his family and my mother. He surprised me and showed up early with grocery bags. He wanted to cook dinner for me. As if he hadn't spent the entire week cooking for his family. Before he started, he poured two glasses of wine and told me to have a seat.

As he held a glass in his hand, I looked up at him then down at the glass. "Stop for a minute."

"What? Is something wrong?"

"Uh, uh…" I put my index finger on his lip. "I want some of this first."

"My pleasure, Ms. Bassett."

I put my arms around his neck and softly pulled him down to meet my lips. "I missed you."

Hayes placed the bottle of wine on the counter and wrapped his arms around me, lifting me out of my seat. "I missed you too."

After putting me down, he quickly reverted to chef mode. "Go sit on the other side of the room, so I can get dinner started."

"Yes, sir."

I sat down at the island in the middle of the kitchen and watched as he cut, chopped, and sautéed. He looked masterful as he cooked.

"Our kids are going to be the only kids on the block with a daddy that loves to cook."

"Nah, I don't think there're going to be any more kids for me; that would be too weird. They would be younger than my grandchildren." He didn't even look up as he spoke.

I stared at him because this was the first that I had ever heard that he wasn't interested in having any more kids. Hearing it, though, knocked the wind out of me for a few seconds.

Hayes finally looked over at me. "You okay? Would you like for me to refresh your drink?"

He wiped his hand on the apron that was tucked in the top of his pants then poured me another glass of wine.

I slowly sipped from my glass. "Thank you. So, you mean, you and I couldn't have one or two kids?"

Hayes walked back over to the stove and put a handful of onions and garlic in a frying pan of hot olive oil. "VJ, I'm getting too old for that."

I watched his back as I listened to the oil sizzle and pop. *Hayes doesn't want any more children? I suppose we've never talked about this before. Maybe I just assumed he'd want to have children with me.*

I was a little stymied by this revelation.

———

"Was your dinner okay?"

I looked down at my plate. "I'm sorry, everything was great. I think I might have had a little too much wine." I stood up to clear the table. "You cooked, so I'll clean."

"Let me help you."

"No, please, you've already done too much. Why don't you go find us a movie or something on TV to watch? I'll rinse the dishes off, wipe the counter down, and load the dishwasher. I'll be in there as soon as I finish."

As I picked his plate up off the table, Hayes grabbed me and held me by my hips. He kissed me and sat back. I smiled and continued on into the kitchen. *Now what? No children? I'm not sure that's a compromise that I'm willing to make. I've always planned to have children. I couldn't imagine marrying him and not having at least one child. Would I be able to settle for just one child, though? Growing up I had a great life, but I hated being an only child. It's still early in our relationship and Hayes could possibly change his mind. Maybe I could even change mine. Who knows? But if there is no chance he'll change his mind…I don't know. I don't know.*

Hayes voice broke my reverie. "You almost finished in there? I found something good for us to watch."

"Yeah, I'll be there in a minute." I took a deep breath and attempted to relax my face.

After walking into the room, I found Hayes on the couch, so I curled up next to him and grabbed his arm and wrapped it around my shoulder.

"So what are we watching?"

"Let's watch 'Big Bang Theory,' something funny."

"That's fine. That is a funny show." I paused for just a moment. "So, Hayes, what did your family think? Did I make a good impression?"

He lowered the remote control and looked down at me. "Of course you did. Why would you think otherwise?"

I just had to put it out there. "Your mother was not at all happy about our relationship. You had to see that."

He took his arm from around me and sat up. "I mean,

it's not you, but you know that, right?"

"Of course not, it's the age thing. I know that. But, Hayes, did you see how disappointed she was last Friday? I admit, she was much better on the 4th, but feelings don't change that quickly."

"You have to see things from her point of view..."

"Oh, I do. That's not a problem. I completely understand your mother's position. I guess, I wasn't prepared, that's all, and that was partially my fault. Everyone had told me not to let my mom and dad's divorce trickle into other areas of my life. Well...I'm off my game." I silently considered if I should bring up the issue about children again. I quickly concluded that now was as good a time as any. "So, Hayes, earlier you said you were done having children..."

"Our children would be younger than my grandchildren."

This conversation was the most difficult conversation I had ever had. I was forming the words in my head, but they were having difficulty getting pass the dryness in my throat. I was also unprepared for the tears I felt stinging my eyes. I was nervous, afraid of what Hayes might say, but I had to know.

"So...but, what about me? I would like to have at least two children. I mean, I don't know that I...maybe as time goes on...with us. I have very strong reservations about having just one child, but would you consider just one?"

Hayes stood up and walked towards the TV then, shaking his head, turned back around. "VJ, sweetheart, I wish I could tell you something different, but I can't. Where is this coming from anyway? Why are we even having this conversation now?"

I was shocked by the sternness of his voice. I wanted to maintain my composure and approach the situation as if there were a legal argument to pose, but, instead, I felt tears uncontrollably running down my cheeks.

"Because I'm 33 years old and I wanted to have children one day." My words came out barely above a whisper.

I was embarrassed that I was unable to control my emotions. I took both of my hands and wiped at the tears, but the more I wiped the more I seemed to cry.

Hayes rushed to my side, but what could he say to change the truth?

"VJ, please don't cry. I don't…please. Here…" He pulled me to my feet and held me close to his chest.

"Hayes…could I just talk to you tomorrow or something? I apologize. I need some time to get myself together. I'll be fine."

"I don't want to leave you like this."

"No, please, I'll be fine. I just need some time alone."

We silently walked to the kitchen to get his keys and then, because he was parked in the garage, I walked behind him to the kitchen door.

Before opening the door he turned around to face me. "VJ, you know, the last thing I want to do is hurt you. I know it's hard for you to believe that I love you because it's only been a couple of months, but I do. I know I can make you happy. I also know we'll have a good life together…"

I put my fingers on his lips. "I know." Then I kissed him softly. "Good night."

———

After Hayes left, I grabbed a glass and the rest of a bottle of wine and turned off all the lights as I went back into the family room and got comfortable on the couch. I needed to find a safe space for my heart, my mind, and my body. The sound on the TV was down low, so I couldn't hear anything that was being said. I wasn't really watching it anyway. This also wasn't one of those times that I wanted to talk, so I didn't call Dee or my mom. I had learned a lot about life, love, marriage, and myself in the last few months. In spite of that, I wasn't quite sure what was going to happen. It had nothing to do with questioning whether or not Hayes loved me. I know he does. Nor did it have anything to do with whether or not I loved him. It was about making decisions that I could possibly later resent him for, and about him compromising what's important to him. I finally meet a man that I can have a good life with, after wasting all of those years with William, and the irony is the man I want has already lived a part of life that I have yet to experience.

Chapter 21

July 9, 2012

Last night was an eye-opener. Actually, the entire week was a lot for me to digest. Last night merely capped it off. Forget that Hayes' mother doesn't care for me for something that I have absolutely no control over. The real problem is that Hayes doesn't want to have any more children. It seems silly that we're even having a discussion about children so early in our relationship, but, the truth is, it's good to get important differences like this out in the open early. I don't have the time to do what I did with William: complacently go along with a relationship because it's the course of least resistance. It may sound silly, but I never gave serious thought to having children with William. It did occur to me, though, if we had ever gotten married we would probably have had children, but I sincerely never gave serious thought to either: marrying him or having his children. Clearly, my issues existed long before earlier this year. I've been living my life in a bubble for the last three or four years. How did I let that happen? And now, with Hayes, I'm looking at all the possibilities that I never gave serious consideration to before. Because of that, I'm faced with a really difficult decision…that has to be made sooner rather than later.

THANKFUL FOR: my eyes finally being opened, even if I don't like what I see

———

I hadn't been at work for 15 minutes when my phone rang. It was Hayes.

I exhaled before picking up the receiver. "Good morning, Mr. Vishmell."

"Good morning, are you okay?" His voice was riddled with concern.

I closed my eyes as I listened to him speak. Unbelievably, I felt tears welling up behind my eyes. I cleared my throat before responding. "I didn't sleep well, but I'm good. I'm okay. How are you this morning?"

"Look, VJ, I want to apologize again for…"

"Hayes, no, that's absolutely unnecessary. And you know what? It's still early, so let's not start our day off by getting embroiled in anything from last night. Okay…" My words involuntarily trailed off.

"Yeah, okay, that's a good idea. Let's meet for lunch then."

I looked down at my Day-Timer, which was splayed open on my desk. "I don't think I'll have time to take a lunch today. Let's plan for an early dinner instead, if that's okay with you?"

"You know what? That's even better. Come by the house when you get off from work and I'll cook something special for dinner."

"Sounds great, Hayes, I guess I'll see you at 5:30, 5:45, or so. I don't want you experimenting on me, though. Okay?" I offered him a solemn chuckle.

"No experiment, but you're going to love it."

"I guess I'll take your word for it. Talk to you later."

As soon as Hayes was off of the line I buzzed my secretary. "Good morning again, Carolyn, would you do me a favor and hold all of my calls today? I'd appreciate that."

"All calls?"

"Yes, ma'am, it doesn't matter who it is. Please take messages. Thank you."

When we finished talking I looked back down at my calendar, which had nothing scheduled for the entire day.

———

By the end of the day I was exhausted from avoiding Hayes. I stayed away from my office as much as I possibly could. I even left my cell phone in my purse, so that I didn't have to speak to anyone. I knew both Hayes and Dee would call my cell phone if I didn't answer their repeated calls to my office. I didn't leave the building for lunch because I didn't want to run into anyone, but I didn't have much of an appetite anyway. At a little after 5 o'clock I crept back to my office to gather my belongings and to head for Hayes' house. Carolyn had left for the day, but not before leaving several messages on my desk. I didn't bother looking at them. What was the point? The voicemail light on my phone was also lit. No point in checking those messages either.

As I pulled out of the parking deck, I checked the voicemail on my cell phone. Of course there were a few messages from Dee. There is a reason why she's my best friend, she's crazy and concerned. Nothing about her has changed from the first day that we became friends; she has always been concerned about my welfare, like a sister. Even though I normally shared everything with her, today was different. I was inside my head and it was the only place I needed to be at the moment – particularly after all of the ranting and raving I had done about my mom and dad. In retrospect, I am very embarrassed about all of that. Not about feeling what I felt, or what I continue to feel, but for the way I acted out. I will apologize to my mom some time soon. It'll be a little while longer before I can offer my dad a similar apology.

As I turned onto Hayes' street I became very anxious in a way that I had never experienced before. I wasn't sure what the night was going to offer but, in spite of the anxiety, I was still a little excited about seeing him. As his house came into view, I smiled at the thought of his cologne. He always smells really great. I turned onto his driveway and, as usual, the garage door was open, awaiting my arrival. After I turned off the ignition I sat in the car for a few seconds. I clutched the steering wheel with both hands and gave myself my trial prep-talk: *You have already won this case for your client. Appearing in court before the judge and jury is just a formality. Stay confident and focused. Make the judge, the jury, and the opposing counsel love you, all the way through "YOUR" winning verdict.* I was ready. Whatever happens tonight happens.

Hayes was standing in the kitchen at the stove when I

walked in, so I walked up behind him, wrapped my arms around him and lay my head on his back as I hugged him.

"I don't know what that is you're stirring, but it smells really good in here."

Hayes stopped what he was doing, turned to face me, and gave me a soft, lingering kiss. "That's how much I missed you today."

I loved when he looked at me the way he was looking at me – like his eyes were remembering me from before.

Placing my hands on either side of his face, I kissed him again.

"Ms. Bassett, you're about to…girl…"

I smiled and walked to the cabinet to get a couple of glasses. "Is it okay if I open a bottle of wine?"

Hayes watched me but didn't say a word.

"Counselor, is it okay if…"

"Of course it is." His eyes smiled. "Something is different about you tonight. I can't put my finger on it."

I turned my back and reached for a bottle of wine in his chiller. "I don't know what you're talking about. White or red, sir?"

"Whatever you decide is fine."

I'm not a fan of the red, so I chose a nice Pinot Grigio. After pouring two glasses of wine, I walked back across the kitchen and leaned up against the counter next to the stove, as Hayes finished preparing our meal. I drank from my glass then held his glass up to his lips.

He took a sip then bent down and kissed me. "I really missed you today."

"I missed you too." I sipped from my glass again. "What time is dinner going to be served?"

"Any minute now, sweetie." He turned and smiled at me before turning his attention back to his special recipe.

"Okay, I'm going to go to the restroom to wash my hands and freshen up a little. I'll be right back."

Hayes turned and watched me as I walked out of the room. Once I was in the bathroom I turned on the faucet and looked at myself in the mirror. *Stay honest, with yourself and with Hayes. No matter what you and he discuss tonight, do not get overly emotional. Stay focused.* I returned to find the table set and our meal served. Hayes had outdone himself. He was right; the meal was special. If he ever left law he could easily open his own catering business.

After dinner we took our second bottle of wine into the family room with us. The TV watched us as Hayes told me about his day. I could hear his voice, but his words somehow eluded me. I was preoccupied...and it showed.

"VJ, did you hear what I said? What are you thinking about?"

"I'm sorry, what were you saying?"

He shook his head. "It was nothing important. You know, you were also a little distant during dinner. What's going on?"

"Nothing..."

"No, it's something. Please talk to me."

I took a sip from my glass and sat it on an end table next to the couch. "Hayes, I want you. I want you more than I've ever wanted any man, and I know you want..."

"I love you, VJ."

I put my hand up to his lips. "I know you love me. I love you too, but I'm 33 years old…and I want babies. I want babies."

Hayes stood to his feet and walked across the room then back over to me. "VJ, I thought…I don't know what I thought. You know we can be happy without having any more children. I don't want to be 70 years old with a child graduating from high school and I don't want a child whose college graduation I might not be here for."

Nodding my head, I stood up and put my arms around him. "I understand that, and you're right. You've had your children. You have grandchildren and it wouldn't make sense for you to have more children. I understand that."

Hayes stepped back from my grasp. "So…what are you saying?"

"It has been a beautiful few months for me. Now I know what love feels like. I know what to expect…what to look for, but you and I both know that…I don't have the right to ask you for something that you can't…that you're unable to give to me. And if I'm honest with myself, I'm not going to change my mind anytime soon about having children." I shrugged my shoulders. "I can't apologize for that."

The pain and disappointment in his eyes was about to break me. I fought back the tears that were surely going to burst through at any moment.

"Please understand that this is the most difficult thing I've ever done in my life. Hayes, I can't begin to tell you how happy you make me; how happy I know we would be together, but I don't ever want to resent you because we didn't have any children together, and I don't want you to ever grow to resent me because, oops, we slipped up and made a baby."

He never said another word to me.

"I'm going to leave." I turned to walk away, but turned back around and kissed him one last time. "I love you, Hayes."

He held me like his life depended on it. I felt my tears break free and run down my cheeks. I gently pushed away from his chest and turned away without looking back at him. I couldn't bear to see how much I had hurt him.

———

July 10, 2012

It's 3 o'clock in the morning and I haven't been asleep yet. I want to call Hayes to see if he's okay, but I know that's not a good idea. Wish I was 12 years old again. Life was a lot less complicated then. I am pretty certain love is not supposed to hurt like this. I don't feel like writing much, just thought I'd write something because I was up. I have a client coming in mid-morning some time, after my appointment with Dr. Hanyard. Going to try to get some sleep...

THANKFUL FOR: the opportunity to know love

Chapter 22

July 10, 2012

I'm absolutely exhausted. I don't know how I'm going to make it through the day. There's no point in drinking any coffee. It won't do a thing to help how I feel. I'm working on about an hour of sleep. I wonder how Hayes slept last night? I could call him and ask, but that seems so hypocritical. But is it? We're both adults. We...I'm not even going to entertain the thought. I did the right thing. I know I did. It wasn't selfish because the decision was already made: I want children and Hayes doesn't. I can't be angry with him for that, but I also can't wait around to see if he changes his mind. Nor am I juvenile enough to believe that just because we agree to have one child that one will be enough, or that we couldn't end up with an unplanned pregnancy. I don't know. The decision doesn't stop me from wanting him, though. He and I waited all that time, just for this to happen.

There's a lot to talk about with Dr. Hanyard today, so surely that'll keep me awake for a while. After that I don't know how I'm going to make it. I'll just have to lock my door and take a nap after my appointments. I better stop writing and get ready to leave the house. I'm moving in slow motion, so it's going to take me a little longer than usual to get myself together.

THANKFUL FOR: the opportunity to say it all out loud

to Dr. Hanyard today

———

"So have a seat, VJ. It's good to see you."

"It's good to see you too, Dr. Hanyard."

Dr. Hanyard sat quietly for a few seconds and watched me as I fumbled with my purse. "How are you? You don't seem like yourself this morning."

"I didn't get much sleep last night. I'm really, really exhausted."

"No, I think it's more than that. What's been going on with you since the last time I saw you?" She sat back and waited for me to speak.

I was so sleepy that I was fidgety. I could barely keep myself together. "Well, let's see, where should I begin? Oh, I met Hayes' parents."

"That had to be a little interesting."

"Psss…that's an understatement." I turned my head and looked over at a pink teddy bear on the floor, propped up against the wall.

"VJ, are you sure you're okay?"

"I am. As I was saying, very much an understatement…" I shook my head. "It was very apparent that his mother didn't approve of me. Well, not me so much as my age. Apparently, Hayes hadn't told anyone that I was 19 years his junior, which I get. I think I understand all of the reasons he might not have. Uhm…but, you know, his father, his brothers, and his sister-in-laws seemed to be okay with the age thing."

Dr. Hanyard looked baffled. "So, was there a big

scene or something, or was it just an uncomfortable situation for you? I sense there's more."

"Initially, it was very uncomfortable. The evening started off with Hayes' father introducing himself to my mother because he thought Hayes was dating her."

Dr. Hanyard chuckled. "Okay, well, yeah, uncomfortable would be one word for that."

"Yeah, but we managed to work through it. Uhm…by the 4th of July things with his mom seemed better, but you know. I understood that it would take her some time to get adjusted…"

"You said understood, past tense." The doctor watched me more than she wrote.

I sighed. "Uhh, we got past that, I guess. Then fast forward to my conversation with Hayes regarding children. I want a few; he doesn't want any more."

Dr. Hanyard didn't speak, but she did look a little disappointed.

"You know, I'm very aware that Hayes and I have only really known each other for a short time, but I'm convinced that he loves me and that I love him. I'm equally as convinced of all the good stuff about him: good provider, good husband, good friend…good lover; and I would do everything in my power to be equally good for him. I don't think that would be difficult at all. But honestly, I want to have babies." I shook my head, as if to shake the disappointment from my mind. "Maybe I'm being selfish. I want the babies and I want him too, but it's clear that I can't have both, and I don't think I'm willing to compromise and say one child is enough; even though that was never on the table. It was just a scenario that crossed my mind."

Dr. Hanyard placed the top of her pen on her lips. "You and he couldn't reach a compromise?"

"No, he was pretty adamant regarding why he didn't want any more children, and the funny thing is I get it. I understand. So, I ended our relationship last night."

"Oh, so this is fresh…brand new. Do you think any of this has anything to do with your parents?"

I frowned. "Oh, absolutely not; at least, not…no, it has nothing to do with that. It's really as simple as I want babies, more than one, and Hayes doesn't want to have any more children. So I accept that. Believe it or not, it's more about my previous relationship than anything else. I wasted all of that time because, truthfully, I was too lazy to invest in the relationship. It was easy and there were no real demands made of me. And, Dr. Hanyard, that was entirely my fault. I don't want to waste any more time. I want to get married and have a few children in the next few years. I'm not that far from forty, you know?"

She nodded her head. "I know. So, where are you with your parents' divorce? Have you talked any more with your mom and dad?"

"All of this with Hayes, you know, the age and baby thing made me think…about everything. With my dad, I kind of came to the conclusion that there's a quiet part of me, not so deep down inside, that wished he liked me, or us, more, but somehow I also don't think it's true that he doesn't like us. Eighteen, nineteen, twenty years is a long time to be with someone and not have any more feelings for them. Daddy was with Mom for 40 years before he made his transition to his, so called, new family…40 years. Really, it made me wonder what goes through a person's mind when they decide to change families, after 40 years. How does that happen? Is there no consideration given to the family that's being left behind? In spite of having those thoughts, I knew that still wasn't what was coming from my core. I think the steady whispers echoing in my soul are, 'Choose me…love me more…'"

Dr. Hanyard smiled. "But you know your father loves you; right?"

"Oh, absolutely, without a shadow of a doubt, I know it's just the little girl in me. I've also been thinking a lot about how ridiculous I acted about everything." Laughing, I continued. "I'm working it out, though."

"It seems like you might be. So…"

"The big issue on my plate right now is Hayes. I love him, but I know we can't be together. Dr. Hanyard, I thought my parents' divorce hurt, but that was nothing compared to how I feel right now." I lowered my head and smiled to myself. "Prior to Hayes, I had been carelessly going on with life like, I don't know, like I was the princess of everything. I blame my dad for that." I laughed at how ridiculous that sounded.

Dr. Hanyard tilted her head to one side and gave me a wide, toothy grin. "VJ, there's no doubt that you're going to be fine. You've had to deal with a lot of uncomfortable situations in the last few months.

Honestly, though, it's just normal life. And you're right, maybe you were going through life with rose-colored glasses on. Maybe you're one of those fortunate people who is somehow able to avoid certain emotional pitfalls in life, and good for you if that's the case."

"Doctor, do you think I did the right thing with Hayes?"

"Only you and he know if it was the right thing." She laid her pen on the pad on her lap, clasped her hands, and sat back in her chair.

———

Back at work, after my first appointment, I locked my office door and turned off the lights. No sooner had I dozed off when there was a very loud knock at my door.

"Vada Jade Bassett, open this doggone door, right now!"

It was Dee.

I slid my hand down my face and slowly walked across the room. She pushed the door open as soon as I unlocked it.

"Why is it so dark in here?" She flipped the light switch on as she spoke. "Whoa, you look horrible. What's wrong with you? Why haven't you answered any of my calls?"

I rolled my eyes and walked back behind my desk to sit down. "Close the door, please."

Dee complied then came and sat on the desk next to me. "For real, what's going on? I called Mama Bassett and she said she didn't know what was going on with you because she hadn't talked with you either. What's up, V?"

I sat down and rested my head on the back of my chair.

Dee threw her hands up in the air. "Well…"

"I broke up with Hayes."

Dee jumped to her feet and swung me around in my chair to face her. "What are you talking about? Why would you break up with him? He got a baby mama or something? He isn't gay is he?"

"Uh, uh, he doesn't want me to be his baby mama."

"What are you talking about?"

I got up and walked over to the love seat in my office and plopped down on it. "We had a long talk and, what can I tell you, I want babies and he doesn't. I'm starting to feel like I sound like a broken record." I lie back on the chair and put my arm over my eyes to block out the light.

"V, that's nothing y'all can't work out…" She sat down on the love seat next to me as she spoke.

"It's just not that easy. Look, Hayes is 52 years old and he doesn't want to have children younger than his grandchildren, and I can't blame him. I'm glad he's smart enough to know that, my dad wasn't."

"Well, your dad doesn't have any…"

I sat up and looked at her. "Don't go there, Dee. Just don't go there. There's nothing funny about this."

"I know. I apologize. So, what are y'all going to do? How did he take this? That man loves you, V."

"What do you mean, what are we going to do? I

ended the relationship. There's no point in either of us pursuing it. What's going to change between now and whenever? He's just going to get older and I'm still going to want children. And to answer your last question, he looked devastated. He didn't say a word to me. Even, now, when I think about the look that was on his face, I can barely take it." I looked away for a second. "Change the subject. I don't want to talk about it anymore."

Dee leaned back against the arm of the love seat. "So, how are y'all going to avoid seeing each other?"

I looked at her and tightened my lips. "How am I going to avoid seeing him? A better question is: How am I going to avoid wanting to see him? Dee, you know me. I have never wanted anyone or anything more than I want Hayes. I have no idea how to do this."

Chapter 23

July 23, 2012

It's been almost two weeks since I've seen or talked with Hayes…because I'm a coward. Everyday I've gone to work and kept my door closed. If he's walking by I don't know anything about it. He hasn't called me. If he were to call, I know I'm not strong enough to ignore him. I wish he would call, though…just so I could know that he's okay. Last night I slept a little better. I volunteered at a day camp yesterday too. The kids kept my mind occupied and I was exhausted when I got home.

I'm going to call my dad this evening. We haven't talked in a while. I would love to see him, too. I could do without seeing LaDonna and the kids, but I guess they're a package deal.

THANKFUL FOR: still feeling butterflies in my stomach when I think of Hayes

---

I was walking in the building when my cell phone rang. I stopped and stuck my hand in my purse to fish it out. I was surprised to see that my dad was calling. *What a coincidence.*

"Hi, Daddy, you must have felt me thinking about you. I was going to call you later today."

It wasn't my daddy.

"Hi, VJ, this is LaDonna."

"Where's my dad?"

"He's in the hospital…"

"What do you mean he's in the hospital? What happened?"

People walked around me as I stood in front of the building trying to figure out what was going on.

"He passed out early this morning and he hasn't regained consciousness."

"Where is he? What hospital is he in?"

I didn't notice it at first, but LaDonna sounded like she had been crying. I shook my head, *No, this can't be happening.*

"What hospital is my dad in, LaDonna?" My adrenaline was now flowing, so I hollered at her.

"Mount Sinai, over here near the house…"

"I'm on my way!"

I hung up without saying goodbye or even asking how she was doing. I could find out about that later. Right now, I had to get across town as quickly as possible in rush hour traffic. As soon as I was back in my car I called Dee.

"Dee, look, something's wrong with Daddy, so I'm on my way to the hospital."

"What do you mean something's wrong?"

I didn't have time for Dee's questions. "Look, I'll call you back when I know more. Would you please call Carolyn and let her know. Tell her I'll call her later. I can't think right now. Just tell her to reschedule anything I have going on today, if possible. If not, get one of the other associates to handle things for me. Thanks, I'll call you later."

"Okay, I'll try to wait to hear back from you."

Next, I made the most logical phone call. "Hi, Mom, Daddy's in the hospital."

"Wait a minute, wait a minute. Let me sit down. I'm just getting in the office. What do you mean your daddy's in the hospital? What happened?"

"I don't know. LaDonna called me and said he passed out this morning and he hasn't regained consciousness. Mom…"

"Vada, calm down, I'm sure everything is going to be all right. What hospital is he in; do you want me to meet you there?"

I started crying. "Mom, what if…"

"Vada, look, you don't know what's going on yet. Just calm down and call me back after you get to the hospital and find out more. Okay?"

"Okay…"

Once I arrived at the hospital, I quickly found where my dad's room was. Apparently, he was brought to the hospital by ambulance early this morning and has been here long enough to get admitted into the hospital. Once I entered his room I realized why. He was still unconscious. He looked much older than he did the last time I saw him. How could I let so much time go by without seeing him? I'm his favorite girl. Well, I was his favorite girl. Now he has the two little ones – my little sister and brother. I gazed at him as he lay motionless in the bed.

I leaned down close to him. "What really happened to you? Weren't you happy? Didn't Mom and I make you happy enough or did you just want more…because you were getting older and you thought starting over would help you recapture your youth?" I stopped thinking long enough to gaze at him closer.

"Who are you? I used to know you. I still love you, though." I reached out and held his lifeless hand.

His eyes opened and I jumped back.

"Daddy?"

He smiled and I saw a familiar twinkle in his eye. "Baby girl, why are you crying?" His eyes then closed as quickly as they opened.

I hurriedly ran out to the nurses' station. "My dad's in room 303 and he opened his eyes. I think it's the first time today."

The nurse looked up at me. "Okay, sweetie, I'll send someone in to check on him."

Her voice was comforting and reassuring. It made me feel like a little girl again.

"Okay, thank you." I turned and rushed back to my dad's bedside.

When the doctor arrived I quickly stepped aside. I watched as my father was poked and prodded. His response was minimal, but substantial, according to the doctor.

The doctor stopped for a moment and turned to face me. "I'm pleased. He's strong. That's always good. I understand this is the most responsive he's been since he arrived." He looked down at the clipboard he was holding. "Mr. Bassett appears to have turned a corner." Stepping away from the bed, the doctor approached me, but not before instructing the nurse to make more frequent visits to monitor my dad's vitals.

"So you think he's going to be okay?" I cocked my head to one side as I spoke.

The doctor smiled and nodded his head as he washed his hands. Turning back around, he extended his hand. "I apologize for not introducing myself when I came in. I'm Dr. Essa."

Even though his firm grasp engulfed my petite, brown, manicured hand, I was still surprised by the softness and warmth of his hand. I found myself looking down at our hands as they were clasped together. When I looked back up, I looked right into his dark eyes.

"I'm sorry, I'm VJ Bassett."

"It's a pleasure meeting you, Ms. Bassett. I think I spoke with your sister after your dad was admitted."

I blushed. "That wasn't my sister."

If what I said caught him by surprise he didn't show it.

"Well, your father's responsiveness could indicate that he's better or it could prove to be inconclusive, but we'll need to monitor him for a few days and run a few more tests. To be perfectly honest with you, Ms. Bassett, we're not really sure what caused your father's syncopal episode. It could be any number of things: hypotension, arrhythmia, cardiac syncope, aortic stenosis. The tests we've already run have come back negative or inconclusive."

As he spoke, I detected a slight accent. I nodded my head affirmatively as he spoke. Is he Islamic, African, or what? When the nurse entered the room she glanced over at us. It was only then that I realized I was still holding the doctor's hand. I blushed as I exchanged glances with the nurse, and then released his hand. When I broke my gaze with the nurse, I don't know why, but I looked down at the doctor's shoes – nice, black, square-toed, leather shoes. I folded my arms across my stomach. The doctor continued to apprise me of my father's condition, without ever acknowledging the nurse's presence or the fact that he had been holding my hand for longer than it was necessary.

"If it's his heart, of course we want to know that as quickly as possible. So that we can make sure he receives the absolute best prognosis."

"Thank you, Dr. Essa. I can't tell you how much I appreciate that."

His eyes seemed to quickly scan my face. "Before I leave, let me give you my card, in the event you have any questions later." His hand searched the right pocket of his lab coat. Unable to find a card, he turned to the nurse. "Amanda, would you do me a quick favor and grab one of my cards from the nurses' station? Thank you."

Nurse Amanda stopped what she was doing and looked up at the doctor, and then at me. "Of course, it'll take me just a second."

The doctor and I watched as she left the room. He then turned his attention back to me, but neither of us said a word. Fortunately, Nurse Amanda stuck to her word and returned within seconds.

"Here are a few cards for you, Dr. Essa." She handed the cards to him and then protectively stood next to him.

"Thanks, Amanda." Grabbing one card from the stack, and placing the rest in his pocket, he handed the lone card to me. "Please, call if you have any questions, any questions at all."

I looked at the card, as if confirming its accuracy. "I will. Thank you again, Dr. Essa. I think I'm going to finish my visit with my father, and then leave so he can get some rest."

I extended my hand to shake the handsome doctor's hand again. When we shook hands this time, there was no mistaking the gentle squeeze he gave my hand. Dr. Essa and Nurse Amanda then left me in the room alone with my dad.

Deflated, but hopeful, I slowly walked over to my dad's bedside. I leaned over and whispered in his ear. "Daddy, I'm going to let you rest, but I'll be back to see you later this evening." I kissed him on the forehead then left the room.

Chapter 24

I went back to work, even though I knew I wasn't going to get much accomplished. The first thing that I did when I returned to work was call Dee.

The phone rang once. "How's Daddy Bassett?"

"Well, he's unconscious…"

"Unconscious, what's going on?"

"Dr. Essa doesn't know yet, but he's sure they'll know something soon, and then they'll go from there."

"Who's Dr. Essa and where are you?"

"I'm in the parking deck about to get out of my car. I couldn't stay at the hospital. There's nothing I can do. I'll go back later this evening. And Dr. Essa is my dad's attending physician."

Dee was beside herself with concern. "Why would you come back to work? Did something happen between you and your dad's wife?"

I reached over to grab my briefcase before responding.

"VJ, you still there?"

"Yeah, just getting out of the car; nothing happened between me and LaDonna. I didn't even see her. I imagine she was in the hospital talking with somebody or with her children somewhere." I paused as I approached the walkway to the building. "Look, I'm going to hang up. Meet me in my office in about 10 minutes."

After ending the call, I put on my game face and

headed for the revolving doors. Once I exited the elevator I went straight to Carolyn to give her an update and to find out what I had missed so far today. She had gotten the call from Dee earlier and had forwarded my calls to a couple of other associates. She had also cleared my calendar for the day. Dee was right. I don't even know why I came back to the office, other than to just catch my breath and get my mind together before going back to the hospital later in the evening. I also wanted to Google some of the terms the doctor used, so that I could ask informed and intelligent questions when I returned.

Dee rounded the corner just as I was entering my office. "VJ…"

"Close the door behind you." I walked in ahead of her and put my purse and my briefcase underneath my desk before sitting down."

Dee closed the door then walked over and sat on my desk. "So what's the game plan? As soon as I finish with my next client I'll be free to go back to the hospital with you."

"I appreciate that, Dee." I watched my monitor as my laptop logged on. "I'm going to look some things up and print out the information, so that I can go back and ask the doctor some questions about my dad's diagnosis and prognosis."

"That's a good idea." Dee paused. "Have you called Hayes?"

I stopped typing and looked up at her. "Why would I do that?"

Dee sat closed lipped and silently admonished me.

I jumped up from my seat and walked around my desk and stood with my back to Dee. "I don't want to be the kind of woman that cries wolf. I ended it with Hayes. I need to leave him alone, so he can work things out the way he needs to work it out."

I could feel the tears coming. I would have called him before I called Dee this morning, but for the fact that I haven't seen or talked to him in two weeks.

I turned and looked at Dee. "What am I supposed to say, 'Oh, hey, my dad's in the hospital, I need you?'"

Still sitting on my desk, but now with her arms folded across her chest, her eyes still scolded me. "Well, yeah, for starters. What's wrong with that? I'm sure both of you could use a hug right about now, and you miss him, don't you? I'm sure he misses you too, V."

I stood in the middle of my office shaking my head and crying, until Dee got up and came over and put her arms around me.

"Dee, I can't lose Daddy and Hayes. That would be too much at one time."

"Call Hayes, V. Just call him. "

I let Dee hug me until I got myself together. She was right. I missed Hayes and I needed him. I needed him to hold me and tell me everything was going to be okay. Dee released me and walked over to my desk.

"Here, girl, clean yourself up." Grabbing some Kleenex, she wiped at my face. "Look, I'm sure Daddy Bassett is going to be okay. Do what you do, girl. Research that information that you mentioned earlier so we can go to the hospital and check on him."

"You're right. I need to do that so I can understand what's going on."

Dee walked toward the door. "So, you okay, at least for right now?"

I nodded my head.

"Okay, I'm going to meet with my 2:30 appointment then as soon as I'm finished I'll be back down here so we can go see Daddy Bassett."

I nodded and smiled. "Thanks, Dee."

She stopped in the doorway and looked back. "Girl, you know family takes care of family."

After she left the office I got to work. When I finished reading up on the possible diagnoses that Dr. Essa had mentioned, I called mom and told her which hospital Daddy was in and asked her if I could meet her there between 4:30 and 5 o'clock.

"So, Mom, he's in room 303. I'll see you there. Are you going to be okay if LaDonna is there? That's the woman he's living with now, you know."

"Oh, I know her name. I'll be fine. The question is: Is she going to be fine with 'me' being there?"

We both laughed.

"I guess that could prove to be a little troubling for her, if you were not the person that you are. Thanks for going to see Daddy."

Mom sucked her teeth. "Girl, please. I'll see you at the hospital in a little while."

No sooner had I hang up the phone when Dee appeared and stood in my doorway. "Okay, close up shop and let's get out of here. I'm going to drive my own car because I'll have to pick up Quincy when I leave the hospital. You cool with that?"

"With what; with you picking your son up?"

"No, silly, with me driving my own car; come on with your crazy self."

"It's probably better that you do drive your car."

We hung up and I logged off my laptop and grabbed my purse and my briefcase. I then stopped by Carolyn's desk and told her I was going back to the hospital and that I would call her tomorrow as soon as I knew something.

Carolyn's motherly eyes coaxed me to silence.

"VJ, I've cleared your calendar for the next couple of days. We'll just play it by ear."

My lips tightened across my face. "Thank you."

"Now go on and check on your father. I'll talk with you soon." Carolyn then stood up and gave me a hug.

———

Once we arrived at the hospital, Dee insisted we stop at the gift shop.

"Let me get Daddy Bassett some flowers before we go upstairs." Grabbing me by the arm, she pulled me into the gift shop with her. "Did you call Hayes?"

I stood behind her and watched as she meticulously picked over the flower arrangements.

"Uh, uh, not yet. hurry up, so we can go."

"Why haven't you called him yet?"

I walked back towards the exit. "Dee, hurry up."

She quickly made her purchase and proudly walked

toward the elevator with her two dozen roses in a beautiful, crystal vase. She waited until we stepped into the elevator to resume her interrogation.

"So when are you going to call Hayes?"

I threw my head back in frustration. "Geesh, Dee, why do you always have to worry someone into submission? I'll call him this evening after I leave the hospital."

She smugly peeked at me through the roses. "Good, thank you!"

When the elevator doors opened we walked past the nurses' station. The same nurse that had called Dr. Essa earlier in the day was still there. She looked up at me and smiled as I continued on to my dad's room. We arrived just as my mother was offering to take both of the kids with her, to give LaDonna an opportunity to talk with the doctors in the room. I was amazed. Surely, if my mom could get over things as well as she had, I could do the same.

Dee whizzed passed me with her flowers and went into the room. She excused herself as she walked by everyone else and put the flowers on the nightstand next to Daddy's bed.

She kissed Daddy on the cheek then gently stroked his face. "Daddy Bassett, you gave us all a bit of a scare. Get yourself together and get out of here, so I don't have to babysit VJ. You know how she can be."

Daddy actually smiled at her.

"We all know VJ has the tendency to dramatize things, so I just wanted to come in and look in your face

244

myself. I'm satisfied, so I'm going to leave these lovely doctors to do whatever it is they have to do to get you well and get you back at home." She kissed him on the cheek again, and then walked back over to the doorway where mom and I were standing.

Dee and I then escorted mom, Monyet, and Mansel, Jr., to a restaurant in the hospital. Dee held Mansel while mom took Monyet to the restroom.

"Your stepmom is kind of cute."

I looked at her, but refused to dignify her sarcasm with a response.

Dee looked down at the baby then over at me. "So this is your brother/son, huh?" She laughed at her own joke.

"Brother/son, really, Dee? And referring to his mother as my stepmom," I rolled my eyes at her.

I gazed at the baby who was oblivious to the repartee between me and Dee. He merely needed to have his carnal needs met and it didn't matter who met those needs. Too the baby, Dee was just as good a body as either me or my mom; all of us were strangers to him.

"Well, he could be your son, but he's your brother, so that makes him your brother/son; right?" She laughed again. Looking down at the baby, she now spoke to him. "Sweetie, I'm your auntie/sister and this lady sitting here with us is your sister/mother."

The baby smiled and cooed as she spoke to him.

"Cut it out, Dee. Here comes Mom."

After Mom sat down she ordered something for Monyet to eat.

Dee stood up and handed the baby to me. "Mama Bassett, it's always good to see you, under any circumstances. I have to leave to pick up Quincy." She leaned over and kissed Mom on the cheek. "VJ, I'll get up with you some time tonight." She then kissed me on the cheek and left the restaurant.

I looked across the table at my mother as she held Monyet. "Mom, you win the prize, hands down."

She knew what I was talking about, but questions were her forte. "What do you mean?"

"You know exactly what I mean, taking LaDonna's children off of her hands like that."

Mom raised one eyebrow as she gave Monyet a drink of water from her glass. "Well, what was I supposed to do? Being angry forever is hard work. I choose to live my life more productively than that." She looked at Monyet then at me. "Y'all look alike, don't you think?"

"Not funny, Mother." I rolled my eyes. "Look, why don't you put Monyet in the chair so I can give the baby to you. I want to go back upstairs to see what's going on with Daddy."

After we got the kids situated, I quickly went back to my dad's room to find out what the doctors had said. As I stepped though the doorway, LaDonna was sitting on the bed with her head on Daddy's chest, as he silently stroked her back and shoulder. I watched for only a few seconds before stepping back into the hallway and standing with my back against the wall. *I guess she really does care about him.* A part of me couldn't stomach what I saw, but the sensible part of me was happy that, at least, she really seemed to genuinely care about him. She wasn't with him for his money. Well, she looked sincere. I don't know how long I stood outside in the hallway before finally getting up the nerve to go back inside the room.

"Hi, LaDonna. Hi, Daddy." I walked over and gave him a kiss on the cheek. I looked over at LaDonna who was now sitting in a chair next to the bed. "It's good to see you alert. What did the doctors say?"

Before responding, LaDonna quickly glanced at my dad. "Your dad is going to have surgery tomorrow morning at 7:30. His cardiac syncope was caused by two of his arteries being about seventy-five percent blocked. They told us it's pretty routine surgery." She reached over and grabbed Daddy's hand as she spoke. "He'll need to get plenty of rest after the surgery, but he should make a full recovery and be back to normal before we know it."

Daddy turned and smiled at her then looked back at me. "The doctors told me to try not to say too much. To just lie here and not exert myself."

I nodded my head. "I understand, Daddy. Okay, I guess I'm going to leave on that note, so that I can get back here early in the morning."

LaDonna looked surprised. "You don't have to come first thing in the morning. I'll be here. I'm going to take the children to my mother's house tonight."

I fought the urge to get an attitude. "It's fine. I'd like to be here for my dad."

For a few seconds there was an awkward silence.

"Look, I'm going to leave you two. I'm sure there are some things you want to talk about before the surgery in the morning." I glanced over at LaDonna. "My mom is down in the restaurant; should I tell her to bring your kids back up here?"

Daddy reached for my hand. "Yes, please, I'd like to see them before they leave."

I kissed his hand. "Okay, Daddy. Good night."

I went back down to the restaurant to help Mom with the kids. When we returned to Daddy's room I stood in the hallway.

"Mom, I'm going to leave. I might come over tonight. I haven't decided yet." I was holding Monyet's hand, so I handed her over to Mom.

"Okay, I'll either see you later or you can give me a call." Mom kissed me on the cheek then turned and walked into the room with the children in tow.

Heck of a lady. She puts me to shame.

———

Once I was back in my car I sat numbly holding my phone. Nervously, I finally called Dee.

"Hey, Dee…"

"Hey, so what's going on with Daddy?"

"Two of his arteries are blocked, so he's going to have surgery in the morning. I'll call you once he's in recovery and we've heard something from the surgeon."

"Okay, so what are you getting ready to do now? You're not going home are you? You shouldn't stay by yourself tonight."

"I know. I'm probably going to spend the night with Mom. This day has really worn me out. Things were pretty scary for a little while. Well, it's still a little troubling, but at least we know what's going on with Dad and what his prognosis is. Look, I'll talk with you tomorrow afternoon, okay?"

"That's cool. Get some rest and don't worry about anything at work. You know Carolyn has taken care of everything. I'll go by her desk in the morning to let her know surgery is scheduled in the morning and that you'll call her some time tomorrow afternoon...after you call me." Dee laughed.

I smiled. "Thanks, Dee."

As I was ending the call I could hear Dee yelling in the background: "Call Hayes!"

Still holding my cell phone, I sat in the parking deck a little while longer. I scrolled through my contacts until I found his name. I slid my finger across it and his phone began to ring.

"Hello?"

"Hi, Hayes, I don't mean to bother you. Are you busy?"

"No, no, it's good to hear from you. Is everything okay?"

"Well, as a matter of fact, Daddy's in the hospital."

"Do you need me to do anything...come to the hospital?"

I could almost hear him putting his shoes on.

"No, I just need to talk. "

"Okay, if that's what you want. Let's talk."

Chapter 25

I decided to spend the night at Mom's house. I was probably going to go there anyway, even before Hayes strongly encouraged it. It was good to hear his voice. I really did feel better after talking with him. We didn't talk about our situation at all. We talked about Dad and Mom. He told me I should have called him sooner. One thing is for sure, talking with him stirred everything up inside of me again. I mean, it's not like anything had completely settled down anyway. Could I give up having children just to be with him? I still don't know about that. After pulling into Mom's driveway I attempted to gather my thoughts before getting out of the car. *I miss Hayes.*

I used my key to enter the house. I knew exactly where my mother was, so I followed the glow of light into the family room. She was sitting on the couch reading a book. The TV was on, but the volume was turned down low.

She looked up at me and placed her book face down on her lap. "Hi, daughter, you okay?"

Too exhausted for tears, I kicked my shoes off and curled up on the couch next to her.

Mom lifted her arm, as if making a safe place for me to huddle.

As I got comfortable, she pulled a soft, wooly throw from the top of the couch and draped it across me. When I found myself waking up, I was alone on the couch. I sat up and braced myself with my hands on either side of me. Grabbing the remote control, I powered the TV off. I then closed my eyes and took a deep breath before standing up. After folding the throw and placing it back on top of the couch, I put my shoes on and walked to the kitchen. I looked at the clock on the wall – 3 o'clock. My mom would be up in a couple of hours, so there was no point in waking her up to tell her I was leaving. I needed to take a shower and change clothes to get back to the hospital by 6 o'clock. While drinking a glass of water, I walked over to a small chalkboard that hung next to the door. I picked up a piece of chalk and twirled it between my fingers as I read some of the brief notes that were already scribbled on the board. At the very bottom, in large letters, I simply wrote: THANKS, MOM. TALK WITH YOU LATER. LOVE YOU!

———

July 24, 2012

It's been a week since Dad's episode and almost a week since his surgery. He was released from the hospital yesterday. He's doing great. LaDonna is going to stay home for the next two weeks to take care of him. I'll drop by tomorrow. I don't want to crowd them. Dad also decided to retire – take it easy, as he says, so he can be around as long as possible for Monyet and Mansel, Jr., or Mony and ML as they affectionately refer to them. Hayes and I have talked a couple more times and we saw each other when he stopped by the hospital to see

Dad. Hayes and I are going to meet for dinner tonight. I don't know what that means yet, but it'll be nice to spend some time with him.

I have an appointment with Dr. Hanyard this afternoon, so I can say some stuff and see what it sounds like out loud. Also, the big event this week is Dee's family reunion this weekend, July 27th thru July 29th. I don't think her family has had one in a couple of years. I'm going to go to the picnic on Saturday. It'll be a nice break. I'm still reeling from all of the dinners earlier this month with Hayes' family.

THANKFUL FOR: Daddy pulling through...support from Hayes...fun this weekend at Dee's family reunion

———

Dr. Hanyard's eyes searched the room. "I think, when it comes to your parents, sometimes ignorance is bliss."

"I don't think it's necessary to know all the worldly things about either one of them. I'm pretty sure it would skew my perception of them. Well, maybe not skew my perception, but at a minimum make them mortal. I don't know if I ever wanted to know them as just 'people.' I never saw them as two people struggling in a marriage and I certainly don't like seeing them now as two divorced people. I only wanted to see them as 'my' loving parents...loving each other."

"You do realize they both love you and, as crazy as it might sound, they could possibly still love each other; right?"

252

"Of course, well, at least for the first part." I threw my head back and chuckled. "...even though I didn't do well at acting like I knew both of them still loved me." I lowered my head and rubbed my eyebrows.

Dr. Hanyard leaned forward and put her hand on my shoulder. "Are you okay?"

I nodded my head.

"What are you thinking about?"

"I don't know. I guess, you know, I've been a little unfair to my father...and in doing that I was unfair to my mother, as well."

Dr. Hanyard scribbled on her notepad. "In what way were you unfair?"

"It was their fight to fight, not mine. It was my mother's issue to deal with and she has done a masterful job of it. It's unfair that she had to spend so much energy worrying about me and taking care of me, too. When I hear myself actually saying that I'm ashamed that I've been so selfish, but even knowing that, it doesn't stop my heart from hurting."

"Well, you're entitled to feel what you feel." Dr. Hanyard softly drummed her pen on her notepad. "Divorce is terrible even under the best of circumstances, especially when children are involved, even adult children. In some situations, you may or may not find that someone needs to reconcile, make amends, or apologize for things that may have been said or done that were out of character or possibly out of line in some way. I'm not saying you, personally, have to do that. That's something you have to determine for yourself.

But closure to the chaos has to be sought in some way at some time. You also have to determine that for yourself, as well." She stopped speaking long enough to offer me a smile. "I wish I could tell you that all of the pain will go away or that you won't have moments where you still mourn the change in your parents' relationship with each other. You will have to find a way to deal with that in a way that yields positive results for you."

I silently nodded my head because I not only understood what she was saying, I also agreed.

"So, Vada, what say you?"

"I'm just taking in everything you said."

———

After my appointment with Dr. Hanyard, I rushed home to shower and change clothes before meeting Hayes at the restaurant. As ridiculous as it sounds, I'm nervous. Dee was excited about my dinner plans with him, and so was Mom. On the way home I called to check on Daddy. I didn't stop by because, well, LaDonna's taking care of him and she had suggested that he not have visitors immediately upon arriving home from the hospital. I have to admit, I rolled my eyes when she said that, but I'm giving her yesterday and today. Tomorrow is another story. I'm going to go by and see my daddy after I get off from work, LaDonna or no LaDonna. I'm not my mom, so she better not push me. It doesn't take much for Dee, so when I told her what LaDonna said she was ready to take her earrings off at the mere idea that LaDonna would tell me not to come by to see him. Again, I'll worry about all of that tomorrow.

After I showered and slathered down in oil, I sprayed on just a hint of perfume before putting on a little black dress and some black, platform pumps. I put on just a little makeup and bumped my hair with a curling iron before heading for the door. I was first date ready, even though this was far from a first date. When I arrived at the restaurant I saw Hayes' little, black Jaguar in the parking lot. The hostess escorted me to a table that was situated such that we would be afforded a slight bit of privacy. Hayes stood when he saw me coming.

"Wow, you look great, VJ. Better than I remember."

I smiled. "It hasn't been that long."

"It feels like it has." He bit his bottom lip as his eyes traveled from my head to my feet. "Where are my manners? Please, let me get your seat for you."

"Why are you looking at me like that? You're making me nervous, as if I'm not nervous enough."

Hayes laughed that laugh that I missed so much. "I'm sorry. First of all, let me say again, you look beautiful. I can't take my eyes off of you. Maybe that speaks to how much I've missed you. Secondly, you can't be any more nervous than I am. I feel like…like I did the first time we had dinner together."

I looked up at the waitress as she stood next to our table with two drinks.

"Oh, I took the liberty of ordering drinks for us, two martinis. I hope you don't mind."

I looked at him for a second. "Not at all, thank you."

The waitress quickly took our orders and left.

Hayes cleared his throat. "How's your dad?"

"He's fine. He's home from the hospital now. I'm pretty certain everything is going to be okay. He has actually decided to retire." I kept my eyes on Hayes as I took a sip from my drink.

"Why are you looking at me like that? What? Is there something on my face?" He reached up and touched his cheek.

I shook my head. "No, I miss looking at you. Hayes, I'm sorry…"

"I'm sorry…"

We both laughed.

"Please, let me go first, VJ. You know, I've been thinking about everything and it occurred to me that I didn't even consider what you might want, but in my defense, I was scared. I'm with this beautiful young woman who, one day, wants to have children with me. That scared me to death. I'm not a young guy anymore. Before we got together, I hadn't considered that having children could be an issue for me – been there, done that, you know. So when it came up…" He stopped and shook his head. "…I deferred to what I had already decided. No more children for me. I honestly expected you to accept it with no questions. Because we had gone along for the last couple of months so agreeable with each other's wants and needs, I sincerely thought you would go along with it."

Just as I reached across the table to touch his hand our waitress returned with our food. I smiled at Hayes and the young waitress as I pulled my hand back and put it in my lap. We briefly halted our conversation until after she served our meals. We both thanked her and waited until after she walked away to begin eating.

"Do you mind if I continue talking while we eat?"

I shook my head. "Uh, uh, go right ahead."

"What I was getting to was, I wasn't sensitive to your needs, VJ, and I apologize for that. I sincerely apologize."

After he had his say we ate quietly, occasionally glancing at each other.

When I was ready to speak I put my fork down and dabbed at my mouth with my napkin.

"I think I've had enough to eat, but you, please, keep eating. Uhm, first of all, I appreciate and I accept your apology. Thank you for that. And I completely understand why you felt the way you felt, but, in spite of that, I still owe you an apology, as well. I guess, I really made the decision on my own to end our relationship, but in your words, 'in my own defense,' I felt like you had made up your mind about not having any, more, children. So, because I knew I was on the other end of the spectrum regarding the issue, I knew we were at an impasse and that, in fact, the decision had been made for us. Okay, having said that, I apologize to you, Hayes, for drawing all the conclusions on my own and not really allowing us to come to a decision together about how we would proceed in our relationship. I really do understand why you feel the way you feel. I didn't think I had the right to impose that on you – insisting that if we're going to be together we have to have children. I also should not have been unwilling to compromise. It wasn't so much that I wasn't willing to compromise; I didn't know if there was a viable compromise for me."

When I had said all I had to say, I sat back in my chair and looked at him. He also had finished eating and sat back in his seat. Apparently, our waitress took this as her cue to return to our table. After removing our empty plates and asking if we would be having dessert, she departed to get our bill. Hayes asked her to give us a few minutes before she returned.

He crossed his arms across his chest and looked down. "So, look, VJ…" he paused then looked up at me. "I love you and I would love to have children with you. Maybe we can have one child. I'm not going to lie to you. I'm still unsettled about that."

"Hmm…that's sweet." I smiled at him. "I appreciate the sentiment, but you and I both know that's not something you really want to do. Do I want to be with you? Of course, and the idea of having one child is a scenario I continue to play over and over in my head. As a matter of fact, that was the compromise that I wondered if I could make. Honestly, I still don't know if I can. I can't promise you that one will be enough." I closed my eyes, but quickly opened them because I didn't want to cry.

Hayes exhaled and ran his hand down his face. "So we're right back where we started. Look, I'm not just going to give you up without a fight. I was before, but I changed my mind." He laughed.

"I appreciate knowing that I'm worth fighting for."

"Well, yeah, you are."

I blushed as he stared at me.

"Okay…" He clapped his hands. "So we started off our relationship pretty quickly; what if we just slow things down a bit?"

I nodded my head. "What does slowing it down mean?"

He shook his head. "I don't know."

"No more vacations together. No more expensive jewelry." I reached across the table. "No more showing off for me."

"Oh, the bracelet…" He laughed from his gut.

"I'm not giving it back, by the way. I really like it." A toothy grin spread across my face.

Still laughing, he now held my hand between both of his hands. "I would never ask for it back. I like the way it looks…so close to your ring finger."

Our waitress returned with the bill and stood by idly before either one of us acknowledged her.

Hayes was still holding my hand and smiling at me when he spoke. "Thank you, ma'am, you can put it on the table."

————

July 24, 2012

It was great having dinner with Hayes. It was good to see him smile and even better to hear him laugh. I missed that. I missed everything about him. Okay, so we're going to slow things down, whatever that means. At least his mother will be happy to know that. I can't imagine that either one of us is going to really change our stance on having children or not having children, or that he'll never be scared about having children younger than his grandchildren. I think we both understand what slowing down really means – "seeing other people." This will be new territory for me. I don't want to date Hayes…and other people, too. Apparently, slowing down did not mean he couldn't ask me if we could do lunch tomorrow. It hurt, but I said no….maybe we can do lunch Friday.

Dee has been blowing up my phone. She's so nosy. She just wants to know how dinner went. I'm going to make her wait until tomorrow. I want to hold on to tonight as long as I can.

FAMILY REUNION IN FOUR MORE DAYS!!!!

THANKFUL FOR: talking to Hayes…seeing Hayes…smelling Hayes

Chapter 26

July 28, 2012

That witch LaDonna would not let me visit my father until yesterday evening. I talked to Daddy every day this week, but I didn't want to stress him out by complaining about his wife. She is not doing a good job of making an ally out of me. By the time I got home last night I was too mad to write anything. It didn't help that I stopped by my mom's and she laughed when I told her what happened. As a matter of fact, she laughed really hard. Ms. Cecilia and some of my mom's other friends were visiting, so I didn't stay long. I didn't stay long because they all laughed at me. I'm not mad, but I owe my mom and Ms. Cecilia big for that. I'm going to blame their behavior on the free-flowing wine at her little soiree.

I talked to Dee last night, but I didn't tell her about LaDonna. She would have gotten off the phone and gone straight to my Dad's house. She is always looking for a fight. If Daddy wasn't recuperating that wouldn't have been such a bad idea.

THANKFUL FOR: finally seeing my dad yesterday and for Dee's family reunion later today

---

Dee just called to tell me they were on their way. The picnic is at Lake Norman, which is about an hour from

Charlotte. She insisted we ride in one car, which was fine with me. The picnic will start with breakfast, and then they have activities scheduled for the kids, as well as the adults. After breakfast the food committee will begin barbecuing and preparing for lunch. Food will then be available for the remainder of the day. Dee had given me an itinerary of the day's events, so I perused it while I waited for her to arrive.

Dee's arrival was announced by the sound of her car horn, which she knows I hate. I didn't want her blowing the horn again, so I quickly grabbed my purse and my extra bag, which contained a blanket, a towel, my swimming suit, and a pair of shorts.

As I approached the car, Dee rolled down her window and yelled, "I hope you're not bringing work in that bag."

I ignored her and opened the back door and hopped in the car. "Hi Mr. Brown, how are you?"

"It's good to see you, VJ."

"Good to see you, too, Mr. Brown. May I ask you a question? Why is your daughter so rude, reaching across you to blow the horn so early in the morning, and then yelling out the window like she's out in the country somewhere? You would think she hasn't had any home training, and I know better than that."

Mr. Brown laughed. "She's always been rude like that. I couldn't beat it out of her."

Dee pinched her daddy's arm. "What kind of daddy are you?"

Mr. Brown turned and looked at me in the back seat.

"See what I mean. Quincy, did you see your mama pinch Pappa?"

"Mommy, stop!" Quincy covered his mouth and laughed.

After I closed my door I turned my attention to him. He was seated next to me in his car seat, so I playfully pinched his thigh. "Look how cute you are today, Quincy."

He turned his head toward the window and continued to laugh as he blushed.

After we got on the highway, the music lulled me, Dee, and Quincy to sleep. It wasn't long before we arrived at Lake Norman. After we parked and began to unload the car, Dee's various family members walked up to help us. There were more hugs and kisses than I knew what to do with, and there was absolutely no way I was going to remember anybody's name. While we were talking to some of Dee's distant cousins, her brother, David, and his wife and kids walked up with Dee's sister, Dacia, and her boyfriend of the day. I hadn't seen Dee's brother and sister in a couple of years. They didn't live in North Carolina and Dee and her father usually travelled to visit them. After an impromptu visit in the parking lot, we all found a nice spot under a tree and unfolded our chairs and spread out our blankets. The family members that were part of the food committee had arrived much earlier and were serving meals as more carloads of family members arrived.

"I don't know about you, VJ, but I'm going to get something for me and Quincy to eat."

Mr. Brown had left us to go look for his parents and his siblings, long before our spot under the tree was situated. As we began to walk towards the pavilion, my phone rang. It was Hayes.

"Well, good morning. To what do I owe this nice surprise?"

"Good morning. I was hoping you didn't have anything planned today…"

"Oh, Hayes, that would have been nice, but I'm already at Lake Norman at Dee's family reunion."

Dee stopped and looked back at me and mouthed, "Tell him to come to Lake Norman."

I frowned and shook my head.

"It was a spur of the moment thought, so maybe tomorrow evening we can have dinner or something."

He sounded a little disappointed, but I think that's what 'slowing down' feels like. I was a little disappointed, too, though. Not so long ago, I would have dropped everything for just a few minutes with him.

"It'll be late when I get home, so I'll call you tomorrow."

After we hung up I slipped my phone in my pocket.

"What was all that frowning and head-shaking about?" Dee had released Quincy's hand and now had her arms folded across her chest.

"It was nothing. I just need to relax today." I waved my hand in the air. "I'm at a family reunion in the park or hadn't you noticed? What?"

"Uh, huh…" Dee turned to walk away but abruptly stopped. "Don't count Hayes completely out yet, V."

I put my arm through hers and began walking towards the food with her. "Trust me, I haven't."

———

The day turned out to be a fabulous. All of the planned activities had been completed. Everyone, including me, had eaten no less than three more times, and that didn't count breakfast. Children were running around screaming and playing. The adults, that weren't napping or talking, were playing cards. Dee was lounging on the blanket next to me.

"Dee, I meant to tell you earlier, your brother still looks good."

"I'm glad he got married a little while after you and I became friends, so I didn't have to worry about you and him getting together. That would have been almost incestuous." She rolled over on her stomach and laughed. "You know he used to like you. I didn't bother telling you because he was younger and because he was nothing but a player."

"You talk so much that you just don't remember telling me. He has turned out to be a great husband, though. We probably would have been good together."

"No, I beg to differ. Trust me, I know my brother. It took him a little while to get to 'good husband.'"

I turned and looked at her. "Oh, okay. On that note, I think I'm going to take a walk down by the lake. You want to come with me?" I stood up and pushed her with my foot.

"Uhh, no, I'll see you when you get back. You must

not have seen me coordinating all those games for the kids. I'm exhausted. Wake me up when you get back."

With that said, I walked down to a quiet part of the lake. I stood and watched the boats for a while then I walked closer to the shoreline and took off my sandals to walk through the water. I didn't want to think about anything, just enjoy the cool water on my feet. I stopped and looked out over the water, until I glanced down and noticed tiny little fish nibbling at my toes. I screamed and ran back on the grass like I had been attacked by an alligator.

As I was running, I looked up and there was a really good looking guy with locs sitting with his back against a large tree watching me. I had no idea how long he had been there, so I calmed down and started walking back towards the picnic area. I knew he had seen me running and screaming like a crazy person. I was embarrassed and didn't know what I was going to say as I got closer to him, but as I approached he started speaking:

Even in her strength she seems vulnerable
Though she hides her vulnerability well
In white, she is beautiful
And it is apparent that she loves deeply
Whoever he is, he knows it too
No matter what happens
She should never be sad
She's only learning the lessons of love

I didn't say anything because I wasn't sure what he was talking about, though he looked me directly in my eyes as he spoke.

"You look very nice in your little, white sundress and bare feet."

I looked down at my dress and bare feet then back up at him. "Thank you."

He smiled as I walked passed him. I looked back to make sure he wasn't following me. He was good looking, but that didn't mean he wasn't crazy.

I made my way back to Dee, but I didn't say anything about the really good looking, yet strange, guy with locs. Though, when we made our last rounds to the dessert table I looked around for him. What did he mean by "…learning the lessons of love"? And even if I was learning some lessons, how would he know?

After the to-go plates were made and the picnic area was cleaned to satisfaction, the cars were packed and hugs were once again shared all around. I wouldn't be joining Dee for the third day of her family reunion, but I had certainly enjoyed myself at the picnic. It was nice to see family enjoying each other's company, even if only for a few days out of the year. Of course, it made me think about my own fractured family, but I didn't want to end my day thinking sad thoughts.

As I was getting in the backseat of the car, I dropped my purse, spilling everything on the ground. Dee was standing nearby so she bent down to help me gather my belongings.

"Girl, thanks again for coming. Now you see why I act the way I act." As she looked up at me she laughed. "I hope you enjoyed yourself."

"Of course I did."

"Well, I know you ate enough, you and me both. We'll be working out for a month to make up for today." Still laughing, she handed me my change purse and a business card. "Who is Dr. Essa?"

"Oh, that was my dad's doctor when he was in the hospital." I fingered the card and looked at it before putting it back in my purse.

"Why do you still have his card?"

"He gave it to me and told me to call him anytime."

Dee perked up when she heard that. "The doctor told you to call him anytime. Is he good looking?"

I laughed. "Yeah, and wears really nice shoes."

"Are you going to call him?"

I looked at her and wrinkled my forehead before getting into the backseat and closing the door.

As we merged into the line of cars that were pulling out of the parking lot, I looked over and saw the guy that I had seen by the lake.

"Hey, Dee, who is that guy standing there with your uncle?"

"Where? Oh, you mean Yoshi? That's his son, my cousin." Then as a matter-of-factly as she says anything else, she continued. "I forgot to tell you, he asked about you earlier in the day?"

"Really? What did he want to know, and why haven't I ever seen him before?"

"He wanted to know who you were." She fiddled with her seatbelt as she spoke. "You know my uncle is, like, a scientist or something and has always travelled and lived overseas. They returned to the states a couple of years ago. It's a bunch of them, like, three boys and two girls: Galen, Mahon, Kaori, Fola, and, of course, Yoshi – who I think is the only one that's not married."

"Hmph…why don't they look like the rest of y'all?"

Dee turned around in her seat and looked back at me. "What? Are you trying to say the rest of my family is unattractive?" Laughing, she hit at me. "That's just the exotic side of my family. Their mom is from some island somewhere. She looks as young as the kids. And all of them are kind of different. Not in a bad way, just kind of real positive, open minded, always happy; you know, different."

As Dee was speaking, Yoshi turned and smiled at me just as we were passing him and his father. I watched him as he watched the car exiting the park.

Dee reached over and hit me on the leg. "Did you hear me?"

"What?"

"If you come to dinner tomorrow I'm sure he'll be there?"

"Who?"

"Yoshi."

"Why would I do that? And anyway, I have plans with Hayes."

Dee turned back around in her seat as we merged onto the highway. "I don't want you to stop seeing Hayes, but you were the one that said y'all were slowing things down. I'm just saying."

I looked out the window as the scenery whizzed by.

"Yeah, I know…"

———

July 28, 2012

Great day at Lake Norman, and the weather was perfect. I'm really glad I went. I hadn't eaten like that in forever. Dee was right; I'm going to have to work out like a fiend. But the food was worth every bite. It was nice to spend time in the fresh air, watching children running around doing all the things kids should do when they're let loose outside. It was also nice watching her family laughing and enjoying each other's company. Highlight of my day? Of course it was Yoshi. Well, it was really what he said to me. How could he know those things without ever talking to me? I really would like to know how long he had been watching me and why he asked about me. I have to figure out a way to find out more about him from Dee, without her making too much of it. I guess I'll figure out something.

Dee called me from the car before she got home. She wanted to know why she didn't remember seeing Dr. Essa when she went to the hospital to see my dad. I told her she was so busy sashaying into the room with her flowers that she overlooked him. She laughed and said she was really falling off her game.

Talked with my dad a little while ago and he sounded like he was doing okay. Even though it's late, I could still hear the kids in the background. Hearing their laughter made me reflect even more on my day. Before Dad and I got off of the phone he told me he forgot to tell me Dr. Essa said he hoped I was doing well. All I could say to that was, "Oh, okay, thanks. Tell him I said hello the next time you have an appointment." What else was I supposed to say?

Going to call my mom before I go to bed. It's late, but she'll still be up, waiting to hear about the interesting parts of the day. Tomorrow I'll see Hayes.

THANKFUL FOR: big fun at Dee's family reunion today...family...and for feeling almost normal again

Chapter 27

I was eating a late breakfast when Hayes called to apologize because he had a change of plans. Apparently, last night some old friends of his showed up from out of town unexpectedly and he wanted to spend some time with them today. I was looking forward to seeing him, but, you know, things happen. He invited me to tag along, but I told him it was probably better if I didn't. We could get together another time. As soon as I got off of the phone with him I called Dee.

"So, what time is dinner tonight?"

"What do you mean? Are you saying what I think you're saying? If you are, we'll be at your house at 5 o'clock."

"Can I even get a word in edgewise? Yes, I'm calling because I'd like to go to dinner with y'all tonight."

"Ooh, this is going to be good."

"What's going to be good?"

"You and Yoshi."

I didn't want it to be obvious that I was interested in seeing him, but it didn't matter what I said at this point.

"Dee…"

"What? You're going to say you're not coming to see Yoshi, but, if you do, I want you to know I am going to call you a liar."

I rolled my eyes and bit on my bottom lip. "Okay, so I'm a little curious. What can I say? And something came up with Hayes, so why not, right?"

"Exactly! Who knows what can happen. And if you're curious, he doesn't have any children, but that brood loves to make babies. Did you see all of the children with his brothers and sisters?"

"Why would I care whether or not they like to make babies?"

"Do I have to spell it out for you? You want kids one day and, just think, you and Yoshi would make beautiful little pups."

I didn't mean to but I started laughing. "You are stupid and you are way ahead of yourself."

"Uh, huh, I know, but I'm glad you're going. We'll see you at 5:00. Oh, wear something cute. Attire is not after five; it's more like business casual, no shorts, t-shirts, or tennis shoes, you know. Wear something cute like you had on yesterday. By the way, you were adorable in that little, white dress. I'm sure that's what turned Yoshi's head."

"Girl, shut-up. I'll see you at 5 o'clock."

After getting off the phone, I spent no less than two hours trying to find a really cute outfit. I settled on a strapless, multi-colored, red, yellow, brown, print dress that stopped right above my knee and some sexy, brown, high-heeled, strappy, leather sandals. I decided to just wear some diamond studs and no necklace, so that I looked more casual than dressy. By the time I was showered and dressed Dee was pulling up. I grabbed my red, bolero jacket and went to the door.

As soon as I opened the door Dee started in on me. "VJ, you look hot. Shoot, y'all might make a baby tonight!" She grabbed me by my hand and slowly spun me around. "Uh, huh, yep, this will definitely get his attention. You look good."

"Dee, I want to say thank you, but you know you always take things a little too far." I pushed her out the door and locked it.

"No, ma'am, you have taken it too far in that dress." Dee pointed at me from my head down to my toes.

Walking ahead of me, she opened the back door of the car. "Please, let me. Daddy, isn't VJ wearing that dress?"

Mr. Brown looked at me and smiled. "You look really nice, VJ, like you're going on a date."

I hesitated and looked at Dee as I got into the car. She shook her head and mouthed: "He doesn't know."

I kissed Quincy after I buckled in. He looked over at me and said, "Pretty, Aunt VJ."

———

After arriving at the Marriott-Charlotte City Center, the car was valet parked and we followed the signs directing us to the Brown Family Reunion Dinner in the Grand Ballroom. It looked like they had decorated for a wedding reception. It was beautiful.

"Dee, do I have to ask whose idea it was to have the dinner here?"

"Of course not, you know it was me. I was on that committee, too," she laughed. "If we're going to do it then we're going to do it right. I wanted it to be worth every penny everybody paid, and I wanted their last night to be spectacular. You know how I do it."

I nodded my head. "Yeah, I do. You did well, friend."

Soft music played as people laughed and cameras flashed throughout the room before dinner, which, by the way, was being served buffet style. After eating with Dee's family at the picnic I understood why she chose a buffet. I didn't say anything to Dee, but I hadn't seen Yoshi yet. I watched as members of the Brown family entered the room, and I paid close attention to everyone in the buffet line. No Yoshi. Everyone was more than halfway through their meals and still no Yoshi.

Dee leaned in close to me as I was eating. "Don't worry. If he's not here yet, he will be. I saw my uncle and aunt, so the rest of their clan is here somewhere."

I wanted to ask her what she was talking about, but I didn't because she knew I was looking for him.

"Am I that obvious?"

"No, not at all, I'm just saying."

A beautiful dessert table was set up while we ate and as soon as dinner was over the DJ began to play dance music. So, those who were ready for dessert could have dessert and those who wanted to dance first could get up and do that, too. I got up to go to the restroom to freshen up my makeup. I didn't want to give up on Yoshi yet, so as soon as I was finished I went back to my seat. One of my favorite songs came on: *Giving You the Best of Me* by Anthony Hamilton. I defy anyone to stay in a bad mood while listening to that song. Just as I had resigned myself to getting up as soon as they did a line dance,

Yoshi appeared.

"Would you like to dance?" He held out his hand.

So I grabbed it and stood up. "As a matter of fact, I would."

"Do you step?"

"Uh, huh, I do."

I followed his lead. He smoothly pulled me close and swayed.

"You don't mind, do you?"

I shook my head.

"I thought you looked good in that white dress, but I didn't know. You look amazing tonight," he whispered in my ear as we danced.

"Thank you."

"I saw you from across the room and couldn't take my eyes off of you."

I reared back a little and looked at him. "Do you always watch people from the perimeter?"

"Uh, uh, just you."

"Oh…"

He released me and took my hand and spun me around to the music. I smiled as I watched him move.

"So, what were you talking about yesterday? Was that a poem you wrote?"

He smiled. "Yes, it was. It came to me as I was watching you…before you ran screaming like a banshee." He looked at me as if to get permission to laugh.

I gave him a toothy grin, giving him permission to do so. "It wasn't quite that bad."

"No, it was pretty bad."

All of his teeth showed as we both laughed. The song began to blend into the next song, so we stopped dancing.

"Can we go somewhere and talk, where it's a little quieter?" His eyes explored my face as he spoke.

If he hadn't asked I'm sure I would have.

"Absolutely, that sounds nice."

The next thing he said, as we walked off the dance floor, caught me off guard.

He looked over at me and smiled. "That's going to be our song, okay?"

He didn't seem to expect a response, so I smiled and turned away.

Initially, we were going to sit in the lobby, but Yoshi asked if we could go for a walk. So we did that instead.

As we were walking, he stopped and extended his hand. "I feel like I already know you, but clearly I don't. My name is Yoshi Brown."

I extended my hand and grasped his. "It's a pleasure meeting you, Yoshi. My name is VJ Bassett."

"What's your whole name?"

"Vada Jade Bassett."

He examined my face as he held my hand. "Vada Jade. I like that. I bet there's a story behind that name."

"As a matter of fact there is. I'll give you the abbreviated version. Mom and Dad drove through Georgia, something happened in a little town called Vada. I'm my daddy's jewel, hence the jade. And there you have it, Vada Jade."

He nodded his head and laughed.

"What about Yoshi? I understand you and all of your siblings have unique names."

"Ahh, so you've been talking about me. I like that."

I smiled, but did not respond.

"Well, as you know, I have two brothers and two sisters and I'm the fourth child. Yoshi is Japanese for better or best; my oldest brother is Galen, which is Greek for healer; my next brother, who is also older than me, is Mahon, which is Celtic for bear; and my sisters are Kaori and Fola, strong and honor."

"It sounds like your parents put a lot of thought into all of your names."

"Yeah, they're very proud of that..." He stopped for a moment. "Is it okay if we keep holding hands as we walk? I really like your energy. It's comfortable."

"Sure..."

Chapter 28

By the time Yoshi and I made it back to the ballroom a lot of the Brown family had cleared out. I was sure Dee had been looking for me and had maybe even called me, though I never heard my phone ring.

Yoshi looked down at me. "I hope we didn't have anyone worried, but if they were it was worth it." His smile was appreciative.

I blushed. "Yeah, it was."

During our walk, we had talked about everything: what we did for a living, he is an occupational therapist and works with children with brain injuries; about my mom and dad's divorce, of which he suggested I allow myself to experience all of the feelings involved, so that I could relinquish them when it was time. We talked about his travels with his family and many of his experiences during those travels. I learned he had a great sense of humor and that he could even sing, he says a little bit, but he's really good. We also agreed that family and children meant a lot. All of this while holding hands and walking around downtown Charlotte.

He also explained the poem to me. He said he couldn't believe I was single, and it was apparent that I was sad, even though I was trying to pretend I wasn't, and that I could only be sad about one thing, love. But he didn't know what kind of love. As it turns out, he was correct; I was still a little sad about my mom and dad, as well as the direction things had taken with Hayes. I didn't mention Hayes' name, nor did Yoshi specifically ask about another man. In spite of that, he was sure that if a breakup was involved everything would be okay because there was no way I would have ended the relationship badly, and if it wasn't okay yet it was only because we hadn't arrived to the end yet. I also learned that he had watched me from the moment he arrived at the picnic. Under different circumstances that would have been a little freaky, but somehow it was okay, because it was him.

Dee walked up wearing a big smile. "I see you guys finally met."

The three of us awkwardly stood in silent for a moment.

Yoshi then turned to me. "Vada Jade Bassett, I enjoyed the time I spent with you tonight. I wish I lived here. In spite of that, I know I'll see you again. I'll give you my number, if that's okay with you, and you can call me when you're ready. I hope that didn't sound arrogant. I'm sure you know what I mean, though."

I put his number in my cell phone.

Dee looked at both of us. "Okay…VJ, I'm going to the car. I'll see you out there. Y'all have me standing here feeling like a third wheel." She reached up and hugged Yoshi. "And it was good seeing you after all of these years. I suppose I won't see you again until the next family reunion or some other special occasion, who knows." She winked at him and then walked away.

Yoshi reached for my hands and put them up to his lips and kissed them. "I hope I hear from you soon."

It would probably be sooner rather than later, but he most likely already knew that.

Tiptoeing, I gave him a single, gentle kiss on the lips. "I'll call."

I briefly gazed in his eyes before turning to walk away. As I left the room I glanced back to see if he was still watching me. With a smile on his face, he was.

loved you thru it all

it was a shock and a devastating blow for me

but

i loved you thru it all

you tore my heart apart

left my emotions reeling

never acknowledging my feelings

told the world you got a new life

...even got yourself a new wife

i knew time would be a teacher, it usually is

i tried not to, but I lay in wait

to pick up your pieces

'cause unlike the others

i only knew to love you thru it all

amid the hurt

the pain

the disdain

the devastation

i did only what I knew to do

begrudgingly, but lovingly,

stand by your side to support you

to be there in case there was a fall

'cause you're my DADDY

and I only know to love you thru it all

ABOUT THE AUTHOR

T.R. Baker is a judicial assistant for a DeKalb County, Georgia, State Court judge. *Daddy's Big Girl is her second novel.* Her debut novel, *Every Time I Close My Eyes*, was re-released in March 2013. She has three more novels waiting in the wings: *Yet to be Determined, Sold Sister,* and *Double Vision,* the sequel to *Every Time I Close My Eyes.*

Follow the author at:

www.simplytrbaker.com
www.simplytrb.blogspot.com
www.facebook.com/tayarbaker2
https://twitter.com/suprtay

Email the author at:

www.simplytrbaker@gmail.com